A nightmare come true!

"Good night," Morgan said to Sally and Jenny in the darkness of the tent.

"Night," they both answered.

Morgan closed her eyes—and was instantly asleep. But her sleep was troubled by dreams—dreams that merged into one another like a nightmare kaleidoscope: a shark swimming at her, jaws open, as she frantically tried to protect the girls and herself; a Maya ruler waving a bloody sword in one hand and carrying a severed head in the other; and then, most vivid of all, a gigantic jaguar, springing at her with a roar, as the girls screamed.

Then Morgan realized her eyes were open.

The tent flap was open, too, and moonlight was streaming in.

And in that moonlight, the head of a jaguar, the claws of a jaguar, the roar of a jaguar, and the screams of Jenny and Sally as the jaguar sprang. . . .

Morgan Swift
and the
Trail of the
Jaguar

By Martine Lesley

Random House 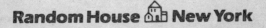 New York

Library of Congress Cataloging in Publication Data: Lesley, Martine. Morgan Swift and the trail of the jaguar. SUMMARY: A Christmas vacation in Mexico with two of her students becomes a working holiday for Morgan Swift when her talents are needed on an archaeological dig that promises to yield exciting new information on the Mayan civilization. 1. Children's stories, American. [1. Adventure and adventurers—Fiction. 2. Mexico—Fiction. 3. Archaeology—Fiction. 4. Mayas—Fiction. 5. Indians of Mexico—Fiction] I. Title. PZ7.L56255Mo 1985 [Fic] 85-2048 ISBN: 0-394-87511-7

Manufactured in the United States of America

1 2 3 4 5 6 7 8 9 0

To Lester, again.

—M.L.

Morgan Swift
and the
Trail of the
Jaguar

Chapter 1

"What did your parents say?" Jenny Wu asked as soon as Sally Jackson answered the phone.

"*Yes,*" said Sally. "And yours?"

"*Yes,*" said Jenny. "All systems are go."

"Fantastic," said Sally.

"I can hardly wait," said Jenny.

"Either can I," said Sally. "Your parents need much convincing?"

"A little," said Jenny. "I had to tell them what a great chance it would be for me to get some sun and swimming, since they're always worrying about me spending so much time reading and doing math. I said if I stayed at home, I'd spend the whole vacation buried in books and risk burnout at an early age."

"I did an opposite number on mine," Sally said. "I told them it would teach me a lot about history and improve my Spanish, two subjects I'm not exactly starring in. Otherwise, I'd waste the holidays on parties and ski trips."

"Of course, I clinched the argument by telling

1

them I wouldn't expect any other Christmas present," said Jenny.

"That goes without saying," said Sally. "No parent can resist *that*."

"Still, it was pretty nice of them," said Jenny.

"I agree," said Sally.

Jenny heard a quick warning knock on her door before it swung open.

"But parents *will* be parents," she said to Sally. "My dad's in the doorway making violent motions for me to get off the phone so he can use it."

"Some people have no respect," said Sally. "See you in school tomorrow."

"See you," said Jenny.

Jenny hung up but didn't go to her desk, even though a tantalizing calculus problem was waiting there. She stayed on her bed, thinking about how lucky she was.

First, she was lucky to have a best friend like Sally. Sally was different from Jenny in a lot of ways. She was head cheerleader at Coolidge High; Jenny was president of the chess club. Sally was into dating; Jenny was into data processing. Sally set the school styles in beauty and fashion; Jenny preferred practical ponytails, faded sweatshirts, and comfortable jeans. But Sally and Jenny were close in the ways that counted. They listened to each other. They respected and liked each other. And they cared about each other.

Next, Jenny was lucky to have a teacher like Morgan B. Swift. Morgan was the best teacher Jenny ever had, better than Jenny ever imagined a teacher could be. Which was to say, Morgan didn't seem like a teacher at all, with her own style of dress, her own style of life, her own style of treating kids. But Morgan definitely was a teacher in the way that counted most. When you were in one of her classes, whether general science or chemistry or physics, or simply in her presence, you wanted to learn all she had to teach, if only to be as much like her as you could.

And right now, Jenny was lucky to be going on a trip with both Sally and Morgan—a piece of luck that was still hard for her to believe, even though they were due to take off in two days, at the beginning of the Christmas vacation.

What made it so hard to believe was that it had all happened so quickly, so casually. But that was the way things usually happened with Morgan Swift.

It had happened the day before, at the end of an after-school physics lab.

Jenny and Sally were the only kids still there.

They had stayed late to finish up an experiment in high-velocity centrifugal force. They were putting on their down jackets and rubber boots to brave the Massachusetts snowstorm raging outside, when Morgan joined them.

She was wearing a down jacket, too, jet black, the same color as her short, almost punk-cut black hair. A silver streak ran through the center of that hair, as startling as her red leather Lucchese boots, though not to those who knew her. Both the streak and the boots were as much a part of Morgan as the golden bee that was always one of the three earrings she wore.

"Brrr," Morgan said, looking out the window at the thickly falling snow. "I know there's a lot to be said for winter, but sometimes it's hard to remember it. I'm looking forward to vacation as much as you kids. I can practically feel the sun on my skin now."

"Where are you going?" Jenny asked.

"The Yucatán—in southern Mexico," said Morgan.

"The weather good there this time of year?" asked Sally.

"The best—hot, dry, and sunny."

"Mmmmm," said Sally. "Good beaches, too, I bet. You'll be able to get a great tan."

4

"I might get a tan—but not on the beach," said Morgan. "I'm really not a beach person. I hate lying still that much when there are so many more interesting things to do."

"Like what?" asked Jenny, who was not a beach person herself.

"Well, there's great diving and snorkeling off the coast, and some wonderful Maya ruins inland," said Morgan. "Not only that, there's going to be an archeological conference in Mérida at the end of the month. Professor Francisco Hernandez—he's a famous authority on the Maya—is going to be speaking on astrology and the ancient Maya, and I really want to hear him."

"Sounds fantastic," said Jenny.

"Sure beats sticking around here," said Sally. "I mean, Christmas is nice and all, but each one is just like the one before."

"I'd sure like to be in your shoes—boots, that is." Jenny grinned.

"Me, too," said Sally.

"Then why don't you come along with me?" Morgan asked, as casually as if she were asking if they wanted to join her for a Coke in the lunchroom.

Both Jenny and Sally had to smile.

"I'm not kidding," Morgan said. "I mean, why not? I'm not interested in leading formal student tours, but I wouldn't mind having you two along. I know you well enough to know you wouldn't be a drag. Besides, I owe you something for the help you gave me."

Morgan was referring to a case involving a crook and a phony cult for kids that Sally and Jenny had helped her expose.° That had been the girls' first experience with how fast Morgan moved, and how fast they had to move to keep up with her. But it hadn't prepared them for this.

"It's so late," said Sally, slightly dazed.

"You have three whole days to get ready," Morgan said. "And my friend Dexter works for the airline. I'm sure he can come up with last-minute tickets. I've tested him often enough."

"It would cost a fortune," said Jenny, shaking her head despite herself.

"Not really," said Morgan. "As one on teacher's pay, I can safely say that. There's a special excursion fare. And in Mexico, living is incredibly cheap—especially if you don't mind tents, buses, and tortillas."

° In *Morgan Swift and the Mindmaster*

6

Sally's face brightened, then fell. "My parents would never allow it."

"Mine, either. They can be so stodgy sometimes," Jenny glumly agreed.

"You never know about parents—especially when you're their kids," said Morgan. "But look, I don't want to push you. It was just an idea that popped into my head."

"Boy, would I love to go," said Sally.

"I'm so far ahead in my schoolwork that I'm practically ready for summer vacation instead of winter," said Jenny. "I'd love to go too."

"When you *really* want something, there's only one thing to do," Morgan advised. "Go for it."

Sitting on the bed, remembering Morgan's words, Jenny felt a glow of achievement, and of anticipation.

She and Sally had gone for it.

And now they were going with Morgan—and wherever you went with Morgan, you might not know what would happen, but you could be sure it wouldn't be dull.

Chapter 2

Morgan Swift was trying to find out what would happen on her trip.

With her bags packed for the Yucatán, she sat at a table in her apartment laying out tarot cards. Her two cats, Twist and Shout, made uneasy by the lightweight luggage standing by the door, were rubbing against her legs and meowing.

Morgan was uneasy too. The nine of pentacles had just turned up, upside down. When the card turned up reversed that way, it was the card of danger, threatening loss from thieves and even loss of life. Its message was "Move with caution."

"Not so good—especially with Sally and Jenny coming along," Morgan said to herself. "Well, these last three cards will tell the story."

She stared at the backs of the three cards still face down on the table. She emptied her mind of all fears, hopes, and speculations so that she could grasp the cards' full meaning when she turned them over.

Suddenly she felt a sharp bite on her right leg, then a nip on her left.

"Twist and Shout," she said. "I know you're angry at me for going away and leaving you here alone—but that nice Mrs. Wilson from downstairs will be coming up here to feed you twice a day. You'll just have to tough it out."

The cats responded instantly. Twist leaped onto the table. Shout followed, chasing Twist across the tabletop. Their racing paws scattered the cards.

Before Morgan could say a word or make a move, the cats were off the table and racing across the room. They came to an abrupt halt in the far corner. Both of them were purring loudly as they began to lick themselves in a self-satisfied way, having made their protest.

"Just for that, no tuna fish treat before I go," said Morgan, with no visible effect, since both cats were making a great show of ignoring her. Then she turned back to the cards on the table. The three cards she had been about to turn over were no longer there. They were on the floor. It was as if the cats had *chosen* to knock those three key cards off the table, which she wouldn't put past them.

She picked up the cards. The Knight of Cups. The King of Cups. The King of Pentacles.

But knowing what they were and what they meant were two different things. Morgan had no idea whether she would have turned them over upright or reversed.

If the Knight of Cups had come up upright, he would have represented the bearer of good news and a beneficial proposition. Reversed, he was a swindler, and any proposition from him was to be avoided like poisoned candy.

If the King of Cups had come up upright, he would have represented a man of wisdom and power, a leader of a high-minded, worldly group or even of a holy order. Reversed, he would still be powerful, but fierce, crafty, violent, and ruthless.

If the King of Pentacles had come up upright, he would have represented a business leader or financier, both honorable and successful. Reversed, he was completely unscrupulous, murderously savage if crossed.

The cards told Morgan nothing—except that she would have to keep her eyes wide open with everyone she and the girls met on this trip.

She would have to keep her eyes open—and hope for one of the bursts of illumination that were her secret gift. She called them flashes, and though she didn't know when to expect them or where they came from, she did know that they let her spot evil and danger, often where she least expected them.

The trouble was, she could not count on a flash coming when she needed one. They were as unpredictable as lightning. Perhaps if she laid out the cards again—

Her doorbell told her it was too late for that.

Sally and Jenny had arrived. Morgan glanced at her watch. They had to hurry if they wanted to make their plane. Boston's Logan Airport was an hour's drive from Langford.

They made it with twenty minutes to spare. Even on icy roads, Morgan's experience as a teenage drag racer paid off.

"You sure can handle that car," said Sally as they left Morgan's vintage Mercedes 190 in the airport parking lot and headed for the departure lounge.

"With anyone else at the wheel, I would have been a little nervous," admitted Jenny. "But not with you. You were in total control. I could feel it."

"Thanks—but maybe I did drive a little too fast," said Morgan. "I have a tough time keeping my speed down. Out west where I learned to drive, you just naturally pressed your foot all the way down on the accelerator—no matter how dangerous it might be."

Morgan was clearly about to add something else, but she stopped. A shadow crossed her face.

Both Sally and Jenny noticed it. They always paid close attention when Morgan made any reference to her past. It was a mystery that the girls hungered to solve.

"You have an accident or something?" asked Jenny.

"Yes," said Morgan, in a voice that did not encourage further questioning.

"Anyone hurt?" asked Sally.

"Yes," said Morgan. Then she said, "Brrr, I'm freezing. I can hardly wait to feel that Caribbean sun." And she quickened her pace toward the departure lounge, moving a few steps ahead of the girls and cutting off conversation.

Sally and Jenny exchanged glances, silently agreeing to store away this latest scrap of information. Then they hurried to keep up with Morgan, who was already going through the airport door.

Four and a half hours later, they followed Morgan through another door. An airplane door. Out into the hot, dazzling sunlight that flooded the airport at Cancun.

Soon after that, they were in the back of a

taxi, heading toward the sea they had spied through the airplane window.

"Hey, I thought you said we were roughing it," said Sally, looking out the taxi window at the long avenue of luxury hotels. "This looks like some kind of fairyland."

"It's more like an adult Disneyland," said Morgan with a small grimace. "About twenty years ago, before my time unfortunately, Cancun was just a tiny, quiet fishing village on the tip of the Yucatán peninsula. Then some people with money saw how much its fine white Caribbean beaches were worth in pesos and dollars. It's amazing how many hotels, cabanas, swimming pools, restaurants, night clubs, golf courses, tennis courts, and gift shops money can build to make more money—and how much natural beauty it can destroy."

"Then what are we doing here?" asked Jenny.

"We're on our way to a better place," said Morgan. "I'm sorry I didn't get a chance to fill you in on all the details of the trip—but the last couple of days were so rushed."

"Don't we know it," said Sally. "You must have had to stay up all night to come up with that midterm physics final. I don't even want to think how I did on it."

"Don't, then," said Morgan. "We're on vacation—and I don't want to hear another word about school until we're back home."

"No problem there," said Sally.

"But where are we going now?" asked Jenny.

"First to that boat," said Morgan. The taxi rolled up to the end of a pier and stopped in front of a small ferry boat rising and falling on a choppy sea. "Come on. Let's get aboard fast. It was due to pull out ten minutes ago. In Mexico that means now."

They had barely made it aboard when the engine began to throb, then came fully and loudly to life. A sailor on the pier cast loose the ship's moorings and leaped aboard. Jenny and Sally followed Morgan to the railing at the prow. A breeze filled with spray spanked their faces as the ferry headed out to sea, nosing through whitecaps.

"You still didn't say where we were going," said Jenny.

"See that shadow on the horizon?" Morgan said.

"Yes."

"It's an island, about three miles away," said Morgan. "Isla Mujeres."

"I can see it," said Sally. "Nice place?"

"It has to be perfect for us." Morgan grinned. "It means the Isle of Women."

14

"Does that mean I have to turn back?" asked a man's voice behind them.

Jenny, Sally, and Morgan wheeled around. It was a man. And what a man.

He was just about the most gorgeous man Sally and Jenny had ever seen—shaggy sun-bleached blond hair, a deeply tanned, superbly handsome face, startling blue eyes, and a tall, athletically lean body, set off by a white T-shirt and faded jeans. His smile turned both girls' knees to water.

But he wasn't looking at them.

His eyes were on Morgan.

"Morgan?" he said. "It is you, isn't it? Hard to believe."

Morgan's eyes were on him, too. But neither he nor the girls could imagine what she saw.

And if they could, they wouldn't believe it.

She didn't see the tall, good-looking guy in front of her.

She saw the gleaming eyes, sharp-fanged jaws, laid-back ears, and long, sleek-muscled body of a jaguar poised to leap.

Instinctively Morgan stiffened, bracing for the crushing impact. Then she relaxed as the vision vanished.

"Tom," she said. "You're right. It *is* hard to believe."

Chapter 3

Morgan introduced him to Jenny and Sally.

"Sally, Jenny, this is Tom Sanders, an old friend."

Later, as they all sat around a table under a palm tree in the garden of a rundown restaurant on Isla Mujeres, she filled the girls in on the details.

"Tom and I knew each other five years ago, in California," Morgan said. "It was my surfing summer. Dawn to dusk on the beach."

"You were really good at it," said Tom, taking a long swallow of Carta Blanca beer straight from the bottle. Morgan was drinking a mixture of coconut milk, rum, and pineapple juice, and the two girls were sticking to Cokes. "You could have been one of the best, if you'd stuck with it. I can still see the way you used to take the biggest breakers and come riding in."

"It *was* fun," said Morgan. "But people move on. Look at you. You were even deeper into it than I was. And here you are. Not much surf in these parts. Switched to snorkeling?"

16

"Not really, though I may do some while I'm here," Tom said. "That summer, after you left, I cut out too. I went to Stanford and got interested in archeology. I wound up getting my master's and my Ph.D. What about you?"

"I went in for science at the University of Colorado," said Morgan. Jenny and Sally were all ears. A bit of Morgan's past was surfacing. "I only got my master's in chemistry, though. I was going to go for my Ph.D., but—" She paused a fraction of a second, then finished up abruptly, "But I didn't." She looked down into her glass and took a long drink of her piña colada through a straw.

"Oh, yeah," said Tom. "Sam. I heard about it through the grapevine."

By now Jenny and Sally were on the edge of their seats. They already knew that there was a mysterious boyfriend in Morgan's past, and now they had his first name. But Morgan quickly dashed their hopes of learning more.

"Enough talk about me," Morgan said. "What about you? What are you doing down here? No digs on this island that I know of."

"I'm laying over here for a couple of days, to get some sea and sun, before I head inland," Tom said.

"Same with us," said Morgan. "After we leave

17

the island, we plan to do the big ruins and a couple of the smaller ones, before we wind up in Mérida. The city is having an archeological conference, and Francisco Hernandez is giving a talk on a new interpretation of the astrological forecasts in the Maya codices. Maybe we'll run into you there, too."

"I'm afraid not, though I hate to miss it," Tom said. "Hernandez is tops in the field. But I'm going to be busy elsewhere."

"A dig?" asked Morgan.

Tom started to answer, then thought better of it. "I can't really say. It's kind of confidential."

"Right," said Morgan, dropping the subject. She believed in other people's right to privacy as much as she believed in her own.

Besides, she was partly relieved at the prospect of not seeing Tom again.

The memory of the jaguar she had seen in her flash was vivid. She had known Tom as a nice guy. Friendly, open, easygoing. But that was five years ago. A lot of things could happen in five years. Good things—and bad.

"But I hope we can see more of each other while we're on the island," said Tom. "That is, if you and your friends don't mind."

"Not at all," Sally assured him. The more she saw of him, the better he looked.

18

"It would be great," Jenny seconded. Not only was this guy good looking, she thought, he also had the kind of mind she'd love to make contact with.

"The ayes have it," said Morgan. "I warn you, though, I plan to put you to work. The girls can use some background in Maya history, and I can use a companion for a little scuba diving."

"At your service," said Tom. He grinned, his eyes crinkling in a way that sent fresh tremors through Sally and Jenny. "When do I begin?"

"Bright and early tomorrow," Morgan said.

She was as good as her word. At seven the next morning Jenny and Sally were shaken awake in their sleeping bags. They opened their eyes to see Morgan standing above them. She was wearing a tank top and running shorts that showed off her slender, long-legged figure to its very best advantage. Tom stood behind her. He was wearing only running shorts, and his tanned body glistened with sweat.

"Get up, sleepyheads," Morgan said. "We've already been for a great run. I'd almost forgotten how sensational it feels to run barefoot on sand."

"And I'd almost forgotten how Morgan can run," Tom said. "You two can get up. As for me, I'm ready to fall down."

"Come on, vacation time is too precious to waste," Morgan said. "We have a lot of great things to do today."

The first thing they did was rent motor scooters in town and ride south on the island's only paved road. Snowbound New England seemed a million miles away as they moved past fine sand beaches gleaming white in the sun and countless palm trees spreading their broad leaves against the cloudless blue sky. The ride was short—the island was only five miles long—and they had to dismount when they reached the base of a rocky cliff on the southern tip.

"The ruins are up here," said Tom, and led the way up a steep and narrow trail. Morgan was close behind him, and the girls did their best to keep up with the quick-climbing pair. Slightly out of breath, Sally and Jenny reached the top and stood beside Tom and Morgan in front of the patched-up stone ruins of a building built long ago.

"We think it was a temple dedicated to Ixchel, the goddess of fertility," said Tom. "The reason that this island is called the Isle of Women is because it used to be a way station for Maya women making pilgrimages to Ixchel's center of worship on Cozumel, a larger island near here."

20

"Built where it is, so high up," said Morgan, "I'd bet this place was used as an astronomical observatory, too."

"Maybe so," said Tom. "The ancient Maya never missed a chance to see as much as they could of the heavens."

"It must have been quite a job, building a place up here," said Jenny, savoring the slightly scary feeling of looking out over the endless, bright blue sea far below.

"The Maya were good at building," said Tom. "For six hundred years they built cities and religious centers over hundreds and hundreds of miles in the Yucatán and Guatemala."

"When did they stop?" asked Sally, trying to imagine what it must have been like to be a woman, standing in this very place, praying for a child.

"About eleven hundred years ago," said Tom.

"What happened? Somebody kill them off?" asked Jenny.

"No," said Tom. "The Maya people kept living. In fact, the people of this region still look a lot like the people pictured in ancient Maya art. But the civilization that produced that art and built temples like this disappeared in the space of a few decades—we're still not sure why."

"A mystery, huh?" said Sally.

"A mystery," agreed Tom. "Just like a lot of the past still is. That's what makes archeology worth the sweat. It's a fantastic feeling when you light up a little bit of that immense darkness."

"Speaking of darkness," said Morgan, "there's a lot to do before sunset." She looked at her watch. "It's almost noon. Let's make it back to town. We can hire a boat and dive into that great-looking water down there."

A couple of hours later Jenny and Sally were gliding happily through the water wearing scuba masks and snorkels, admiring swarms of iridescent fish and elaborate coral formations.

At the same time, Morgan and Tom, in rubber wet suits with Aqua-Lungs and air tanks, Morgan's rented and Tom's his own, were heading far deeper. Morgan led the way down. Her eyes drank in the extraordinary clearness of the pale green water, which grew only slightly darker as she moved closer to the sea bottom. Then she saw what she was hunting for—the hull of a ship resting on the sandy floor.

She told Sally and Jenny about it when they were all back on board the boat.

"It's the wreck of a pirate ship," she said. "About three hundred years old."

"Pirates?" said Sally. "This island does have quite a history."

"Think there's any treasure to be picked up?" said Jenny.

"Who knows?" said Tom. "It might be worth hunting for."

"I know what I'm hunting for right now," said Morgan, picking up a spear gun. "Dinner."

"Last one in has to clean the fish," said Tom, and he grabbed another spear gun.

But Morgan was already over the side and below the surface.

An hour later Tom proved to be an expert at cleaning fish with his Swiss army knife. Morgan built a fire out of driftwood on the tiny, deserted beach they had found. And Sally and Jenny sharpened branches snapped from trees to make cooking stakes.

Their hired boat had dropped them there and would return after sunset to pick them up. For the time being, they could make believe they were marooned on a desert island. Looking at Tom, both Sally and Jenny thought there was no one they would rather be marooned on a desert island with. In fact, much as they liked each other, and much as they practically worshipped Morgan, neither of them would have minded being totally alone right now with Tom in this deliciously romantic spot.

"This is simply super," Jenny said as they sat around the fire eating the sweet, tender fish with their fingers.

"It's like there isn't another soul in the world," said Sally, stretching out in the fading warmth of the sun.

Then Morgan said, "I hate to contradict you, but we've got company."

The others followed her gaze seaward. A large white yacht was coming to anchor a few hundred yards from shore, and figures on deck were lowering a dinghy over the side.

"What a time for strangers to show up," said Sally with a grimace.

"Think they're pirates?" Jenny joked, though she wasn't happy to see the intruders, either.

"I know who they are," said Tom. He rose and waved to the approaching dinghy. Two sailors were in it, one near the prow, checking for rocks, the other aft, managing the outboard motor.

"Who?" Morgan asked.

She tried to keep the urgency out of her voice. She didn't want to betray what she had seen when she first spotted the yacht.

Another flash.

This one did not show a jaguar about to leap.

This time Morgan saw a great white shark about to strike.

Chapter 4

"Who *are* they?" Morgan repeated as her vision cleared. She watched the two men rowing toward shore in the dinghy.

But Tom was already moving toward the water's edge to help the men beach the boat.

Morgan and the two girls followed him.

"Hi," Tom said to the men. "How did you find me here?"

"We found the guy who rented you the boat," said one of the men, a big, powerfully built fellow with a bald head tanned deep brown. "He told us he dropped you off here."

"We told him we'd pick you up, and paid him off," said his companion, short, wiry, longhaired, and bearded.

Both men were dressed like sailors, but Morgan had the feeling that was not their real trade. There was something disturbing about them, something slightly menacing. Or maybe, she thought, trying to be fair, it was just that split-second vision of the shark that was coloring her reaction. She'd have to wait and see, keep her eyes wide open.

"We're in luck," Tom said to her. "Looks like we're sailing back to town in style."

"But who *are* they?" Morgan asked yet again as they went to gather up their things.

"They work for my boss—the guy who owns the yacht," said Tom.

"And who's he?" asked Morgan.

"You'll see," said Tom. "I'll let him introduce himself when we get on board."

Morgan did pick up one bit of information, though, before they reached the yacht. As the dinghy neared it, she read the name painted on the prow.

The Shark.

It was an easy explanation for what she had seen in her flash. Too easy for her to feel comfortable with it.

When she saw the ship's master waiting for them as they climbed up the rope ladder and onto the deck, Morgan was uneasier still.

He reeked of money and power, though at the moment he was wearing only a bathing suit on a body softened by good living, and a pearl-gray cowboy hat that must have cost several hundred dollars.

Morgan would have bet that he owned a pair of Lucchese boots even more elegant than her own. And she was sure that when he spoke, he would have a Texas accent.

She was right about his accent at least. Though his eyes registered sharp surprise when he saw Morgan and the girls, his words came out in an easygoing Texas drawl. "My, my, three lovely ladies. To what do we owe this unexpected pleasure, Tom?"

"Meet Morgan Swift, an old pal of mine," said Tom. "She's a teacher, and Sally and Jenny are two students of hers." Then he introduced the smiling Texan. "Meet my archeological angel, Mr. Raider."

"Elijah Zacharias Raider," the Texan said. "My folks were great ones for reading the Good Book. But most folk just call me E. Z. Raider. My friends call me E. Z."

"Why are you here this soon, E. Z.?" Tom asked. "We weren't supposed to rendezvous until Matthews got here—three days from now."

"There's been some trouble with Matthews," said E. Z. "I have to talk to you about it—in private." He turned to Morgan and the girls. "You'll have to excuse us, ladies. Won't take but a few minutes. Look over the ship, and ask the crew for any refreshment you might want."

Tom and E. Z. went below, and Morgan and the girls settled into deck chairs to watch the last of the sunset. The sun was a brilliant orange ball dipping below the horizon. The sky was deep purple and the sea was lavender, with a line of orange light running along the water like a highway toward the sun. As they took it all in, a white-coated steward appeared with a tray of tall glasses of lemonade.

"Made with purified water," he assured them.

"And you said we'd be roughing it," Jenny said to Morgan.

"Wait until I tell the crowd at school," said Sally. "This yacht makes the ones on Cape Cod look sick."

"That's the great thing about traveling—you never know what you'll run into," said Morgan.

But though she kept her tone light, she was wondering: What *had* they run into?

She never really trusted people like E. Z., who could buy anything and everything they ever wanted whenever the mood struck them. She couldn't see what Tom was doing with him, unless E. Z. had somehow bought Tom as well. And if he had bought Tom, why had he done it? Men like E. Z. didn't throw their money away.

Tom returned to deck alone.

"Morgan, would you mind joining us below?" he asked. "The girls can wait up here. Sally, Jenny, there's a VCR and a stereo installed aft. You can check it out."

"Right," said Sally.

"This gets harder and harder to take," said Jenny, already on her way.

When Morgan entered the stateroom below, she felt as if she had been transported from a yacht in the Caribbean to a conference room in a corporate office building. The room was dominated by a long oak table, and by the large screen of a computer terminal that sat on one end of it.

E. Z. Raider, though, was still dressed for comfort. He had changed out of his bathing suit, but only to put on a florid red and yellow Hawaiian shirt, white ducks, and sandals.

"Sorry to have kept you waiting so long," E. Z. said. "We had an important matter to discuss."

"No bad news, I hope," said Morgan.

"Some—but maybe good news, too," said Tom. "Should I be the one to tell her, E. Z.?"

"Go ahead," said E. Z. "You're running this show. I'm just the fellow putting up the money."

"The guy we mentioned, Matthews, is a

chemist," Tom explained. "He was supposed to join us on a dig. I needed him for some thermoluminescence testing. You know what that is, don't you, Morgan?"

"Sure," said Morgan. "It's a new method of dating pottery. You take a flake off the surface, heat it, and date it through the intensity of the glow that key chemical elements give off."

"I figured you'd know about it," said Tom. "As soon as I heard you were into chemistry, I was sure you'd be *way* into it. I know you, Morgan."

"Actually, I did some of that testing on a dig in Colorado two summers ago," Morgan said. "Most of my work, though, was in geographical placing. You know, matching trace elements in the baked clay of pottery with the composition of the soil in different regions of the country to find out where the pottery was produced. We found a jar in the Rockies that came all the way from New England. Seems there were trade routes crossing America a thousand years ago."

Tom turned to E. Z. "I told you she'd be perfect."

"That just leaves us with one question," said E. Z. "Will she do it?"

"Do what?" Morgan asked.

"E. Z. just got news that Matthews broke his leg in an auto accident," said Tom. "That leaves me short a chemist just when I need one. I've got a slew of pottery I want checked out before I make the public announcement of my find. I want to have as much support for my theories as I can. When my scientific colleagues spot an error, they jump on it like hungry animals."

"Then your dig is still a secret," said Morgan.

"That's right," said Tom. "It saves wasting time and energy dealing with the government and the press. Not to mention providing security against looters. As soon as they get wind of a big find, they come swarming in. That's why we've kept this project so quiet."

"And that's why anyone going on it has to keep it top secret too," said E. Z., looking hard at Morgan.

"For a while, at least," said Tom. "One more big push, a few more pieces in place, and we'll let the world know about it. We can't keep it under our hats much longer anyway. We've been at it two years, and that's about par for the course as far as concealment goes."

"But until we do make that announcement, it stays top secret," E. Z. repeated. "There's a lot of greed loose in this world of ours. Being in the oil business, I know that better than most people. Makes me ashamed, sometimes, to be associated with some of the sharks I have to deal with. That's one of the reasons I'm backing this project—to prove that all oilmen aren't like that."

It was Morgan who felt ashamed now. She had let her automatic prejudice against Texas millionaires color her opinion of E. Z. As a scientist, she should demand proof that her hunches were correct, and E. Z. was proving just the opposite. She'd have to give him the benefit of the doubt—though she had to admit, a bit of that doubt still lingered, as insubstantial yet disquieting as a hint of smoke in the air.

"Well, what do you say?" said Tom.

"You're asking me to go on the dig?" said Morgan.

"You've got it," said Tom, with his most winning grin.

"I can only work for two weeks," said Morgan. "Then I have to go back to teaching."

"No problem," said Tom. "The pottery is all lined up, waiting to be analyzed."

"And then there's Jenny and Sally," said Morgan, beginning to feel torn. The idea of an exploration of the unknown drew her like a magnet—it was the kind of lure she loved. But she had promised to give Sally and Jenny a tour of the Yucatán—and Morgan believed in keeping promises.

"It would be a great experience for them," said Tom.

Morgan looked at him and remembered the flash of the jaguar she had seen. She looked at E. Z. and remembered the shark. If she were alone, she'd be willing to take a chance that her flashes had been wrong. But the kids changed things. She was responsible for them.

"I don't know . . ." she said.

"I've got a simple solution," said E. Z. "I'll take care of paying for a guided tour of the Yucatán for them by air-conditioned Cadillac. Then for the last part of their vacation, I'll get them a fine room at one of the best beach hotels, where they can get great tans and meet a bunch of college boys. That should make them happy as pigs in a supermarket, if you'll pardon the expression."

"But that's nothing compared to being on a real dig," said Tom.

"I can't see trusting a couple of kids to keep quiet about something like this," said E. Z., shaking his head.

"But that really wouldn't matter," said Tom.

"By the time they got back home, we'd be close to releasing the news ourselves."

"Anyway, clearly Miss Swift doesn't want them tagging along," said E. Z. "I'm sure she wouldn't mind getting away from her students for a while, if she knew they were being well taken care of."

"I *invited* them to come down here with me—I like seeing kids learn things," said Morgan. "And I *don't* like making up their minds for them. Let's go ask them what they want to do, and I'll go along with their decision. But I want to make one thing clear. If they want to go on the dig, they go, or I don't. I'm not going to dump them."

"You drive a hard bargain, little lady, but I agree," said E. Z. "Besides, I'm sure they won't have any trouble deciding, after they hear the tour I'm willing to pay for. I'll even throw in a few extras, like new wardrobes. There are some fancy shops in Cancun."

E. Z. was right about one thing: Jenny and Sally had no trouble deciding what they wanted to do.

All they did was ask Morgan, "You're definitely going on the dig?"

"It's an opportunity I can't pass up," said Morgan. "But I warn you, there's nothing glamorous about a dig. When I tell you you'll be roughing it, this time I really mean it."

"And you're going too?" Sally asked Tom.

"Wild horses wouldn't keep me away," said Tom. "It's my baby and I love it. But I warn you, there'll be no other young people around— and you'll be expected to do your share of the work. I mean, I can use all the help I can get, but this is your vacation."

Jenny answered for both of them. "When do we leave?" she asked.

Tom flashed them a smile that assured them they had made the right choice.

E. Z. wasn't smiling, though, and his voice made Morgan feel a fresh wave of disquiet.

"We leave first thing tomorrow morning," he said coldly, his voice devoid of all its former drawling charm. "And if you change your mind before then, don't be bashful about fessing up. My offer of a paid-in-full dream vacation still holds. Once we take off for the jungle, there's no turning back."

"Come on, don't be mad just because you guessed wrong about the girls," said Tom, still smiling. "I knew they were made of the right stuff. If they're with Morgan, they have to be."

Almost despite herself, Morgan found herself

taking E. Z.'s side. "You should think it over," she said to Sally and Jenny. "It might not be a picnic you're going on."

"Morgan, your job must be getting to you," said Tom. "I never thought I'd hear *you* talking like a cautious schoolteacher."

"Right," said Jenny. "You're always saying how we should explore the unknown."

"*If* you can handle what you find," said Morgan.

"And how do we find out unless we try?" said Sally.

Morgan gave up with a shrug. It was hard to battle her own words.

"Okay, you win," she said, and saw E. Z. shrug too, though not in surrender. It was as if he was abandoning them to their own foolishness.

"We all win—a great trip to a great dig," said Tom, too pleased by the prospect of the next day to take in what was going on around him at the moment. "This calls for a little ceremony."

He reached into his knapsack and pulled out a cardboard box. He opened it and uncovered an object that had been carefully wrapped in several layers of cotton cloth. It was a piece of carved jade the size of a small fist.

"It's real unprofessional of me to carry this around," he said. "But it was my first find on the dig, and it's become my good luck piece. In archeology, you can have all the skill you want, and you still need luck. Let's all touch it."

"What *is* it?" asked Jenny as she put her fingers on its cold surface.

"Looks like some kind of claw," said Sally, touching it in turn.

Morgan touched it too, but the shiver that ran through her didn't come from the cold stone. It came from a chilling certainty of what the ancient carved jade fragment was.

"Good eye—it *is* a claw," Tom said. "The claw of a giant jaguar, lord of the underworld."

Chapter 5

Morgan looked out the window of the plane that was flying them across the Yucatán peninsula to E. Z. Raider's oil company headquarters near the Mexican town of Villahermosa. From there they would take a helicopter to the site of the dig, deep in the jungle.

Below them were spacious grasslands, fenced into vast squares of land and dotted with herds of cattle and horses.

"I see a cowboy," said Sally, sitting beside Morgan and craning her neck to get a better view.

"We're going over Chiapas province," said Morgan. "It's the Mexican version of the Wild West, practically like it was in our country a hundred years ago."

"Except that it's changing fast now," said E. Z., who was sitting behind them. "The twentieth century arrived with a great big rush when they struck oil around Villahermosa. Wait until you see my company headquarters. It's as near to the twenty-first century as I could make it."

The plane came down low over the high wire fence surrounding the Raider Oil Company and made a smooth landing on the well-cared-for landing strip. Morgan and the girls followed Tom, E. Z., and four of E. Z.'s men out of the plane, and were hit in the face by a combination of tropical heat, airplane exhaust, and refinery oil fumes. But five minutes later they were in the pure, cool air of the headquarters building, protected by thick glass from the eye-watering inferno outside.

Waving a friendly greeting to respectful employees, E. Z. led his companions into his gray-plush and chrome office.

"I'll show you where we're heading," he said, and punched a command into the computer near his huge desk. Instantly, a beautifully clear color photo appeared on the monitor. Like an eye peeking through the thick jungle foliage, it brought into view a towering pyramid of crumbling stone and a series of hill-like mounds, overgrown with trees and shrubbery.

"This is a blowup of a photo taken by a satellite," E. Z. said. "Originally it was commissioned by my outfit for oil exploration. But as soon as I saw it, I knew we had stumbled onto something even more valuable—from a scientific point of view, of course. That's when I brought Tom into the picture." He patted Tom fondly on the shoulder. "I figured that modern technology could give a real shot in the arm to archeological investigation, and I didn't want to hand this find over to anyone old-fashioned. I wanted someone young and up-to-date, like Tom here."

"I was lucky," said Tom. "I had just published a paper on the potential uses of computers in excavations, and somebody on E. Z.'s search committee read it."

"It was lucky for all of us," E. Z. said. "I may have supplied the hardware, but you knew what to do with it. You've made sensational progress, Tom."

"Five years' work in less than two," said Tom. "But I don't want to boast. I'll let the dig speak for itself. Your eyes are going to pop out of your head."

His face was lit by enthusiasm—the same kind of enthusiasm Morgan remembered seeing when he rode the breakers at Santa Monica. She very much wanted to believe he was still the nice guy she had known then. Maybe the jaguar she had seen came from the jade claw he carried, and from nothing else. But somehow she couldn't

dismiss that vision of snarling danger so easily—
especially when she saw Jenny and Sally gazing
enraptured at Tom's handsome face. If any danger was coming from Tom's direction, she'd
have to keep her eyes open not only for herself,
but for them as well.

But on the helicopter trip to the site, there
was no way she could use her eyes.

As soon as they climbed into the large, twin-
bladed chopper, E. Z. ordered that she and the
girls be blindfolded.

"Not that we don't trust you all," he said.
"But there are folks who would play real rough
to find out the location of the dig. We can't be
absolutely sure when we're going to make it
public, and until we do, it's safer for you not to
know anything."

"Security is E. Z.'s department," said Tom, a
little apologetically. "And he's probably right.
Wait until you see the stuff we've discovered,
and you'll understand why we're being so care-
ful."

Any objections Morgan and the girls had were
drowned out in the roar of the helicopter en-
gines.

The blindfolds did not come off until the din
stopped and the chopper had landed.

Morgan looked out the window and saw that they were on a landing pad in the center of a large clearing bulldozed out of the jungle. The clearing was a hive of activity: Indian laborers in white shorts and shirts, many with wide-brimmed straw sombreros, were digging trenches and hauling debris; a dozen North Americans in jeans and grimy T-shirts were running bulldozers, steam shovels, and forklifts; and several in tan uniforms strolled around watchfully, pistols in their belt holsters, rifles in their hands.

"Well, here we are," said Tom as they all climbed out. "Take a look."

They stood before the towering pyramid of crumbling stone they had seen in the photo. Around them, as far as they could see, were remnants of other buildings that had been uncovered when the deposits of earth and plant life hiding them had been stripped away.

"Gee, it's very ... impressive," said Sally, trying to sound as awed as Tom clearly expected her to be.

"Yeah," agreed Jenny, in the same unconvincing tone.

"You two aren't looking at the site with an archeologist's eye," Morgan told them. "Ruins always look like this before they're reconstructed to let the public see what they were really like." She turned to Tom. "I can see why you're so excited. It is a great find."

"This is nothing compared to what else I have to show you," Tom assured her. "It'll really knock your eyes out—and the kids, too. Right now, though, I'll show you your tent."

"I have to apologize for your accommodations, ladies," said E. Z. "We had to devote most of our resources to getting in our equipment and housing it. We humans had to take second place." He led Morgan and the girls to a large tent on the edge of the clearing. "We've put plenty of mosquito netting over the entrance— but you'll have to be on your guard against lizards and snakes."

"Lizards?" said Sally.

"Snakes?" said Jenny.

"I don't want to kid you about certain hardships here," said E. Z. "And remember, if you change your mind, you can still go back. That's one of the reasons I blindfolded you. So you wouldn't be tied to this project in any way if you decided to cut loose from it."

"I'm sure the kids don't mind a few little animals," said Tom. "Right, kids?"

44

"Err . . . right," said Sally, after a quick glance at the ground near her feet to make sure nothing was crawling there.

"Sure," said Jenny, deciding not to ask if the snakes around here were large or small. She didn't want to know.

But there was one fear both of them had to admit when they were alone with Morgan inside the tent.

"I hate the feeling of not knowing where I am," Jenny said.

"Yeah, being lost is the scariest feeling there is," said Sally.

"We're not totally lost," said Morgan. "I place us on the southern edge of Mexico, in the highlands near Guatemala."

"How do you figure that?" asked Sally, though she was really not surprised. In fact, she would have been surprised if Morgan did *not* know where they were.

"You manage to get around your blindfold?" asked Jenny.

"No, but I did get a chance to glance at the helicoptor's instrument panel before the blindfold went on, and then at my watch," Morgan said. "Figuring we were traveling at the chopper's maximum speed, which is a good bet considering the hurry E. Z. and Tom are in, I calculate we covered about two hundred miles in our flight time. And our direction had to be toward the unmapped jungles in the highlands. That's the only place a dig like this could be kept secret. Planes almost never fly over here, and the local Indians keep to themselves. A lot of them don't even speak Spanish."

"What do they speak?" asked Jenny, wishing she had a notebook handy. Morgan came out with the most intriguing facts at the most unexpected times.

"Tzotzil, the language of their ancient Maya ancestors," Morgan said. "They're the last of the pure Maya. We call them the Lacandones. They call themselves the Hach Uinic. The True People. True to the ancient ways."

"They still do things like the ancient Maya?" Sally asked.

"Right," said Morgan. "They have many of the same social habits and religious rites. They live in the same kinds of huts, sleep in the same kind of hammocks, hunt with the same kind of weapons, sail in the same kind of burned-out log canoes. And there's probably a lot more we don't know about. As I said, they're very secretive."

"It's spooky—like they're ghosts," said Jenny.

"They're very much alive," said Morgan. "In fact, you just saw some of them, working on the dig."

"They're not *that* ancient then," said Sally. "I saw one with a transistor radio."

"Their isolation is beginning to crumble," said Morgan. "Modern civilization is doing what everyone from the old Spanish missionaries to the current Mexican government hasn't been able to do—make the Lacandones like everyone else. I suppose in a few decades their way of life may disappear—like the civilization their ancestors created disappeared a thousand years ago."

Jenny and Sally had a bunch of other questions to ask about this strange world they had dropped into—but then they heard Tom calling them from outside the tent. "Come on! I've got a lot to show you."

He led Morgan and the girls across the clearing to a brand-new one-story building. Air conditioners hummed in its screened windows, and a large electric generator throbbed beside it.

"It's a prefab," said Tom. "We flew it in in pieces."

"No chance of our bunking here, I guess," Sally said.

"Not even E. Z. gets to do that," said Tom. "This place is reserved for more important guests—and it's filled almost to capacity."

A tall man with a drooping mustache was guarding the door with his rifle at the ready. A nod from Tom, and he swung the door open.

"You won't believe your eyes," Tom said. "And I've got a special surprise that I've kept secret for you, Morgan."

The surprise hit Morgan as soon as she stepped through the doorway.

It came in a flash.

There, standing in the room, facing her, was an ancient Maya ruler, a sword in one hand, a severed head in the other.

Chapter 6

Morgan blinked, the vision vanished, and Morgan heard Tom say, "Morgan, meet Professor Francisco Hernandez. Professor, Morgan Swift, an admirer of yours."

Before Morgan was a man who could have been the twin of the Maya ruler she had just seen. He was the same size, not more than five feet three. He had the same brown-skinned features, with the same imperious hooked nose, the same obsidian eyes. But this man wore no bright feathered crown or brilliantly colored robe. Dressed in an immaculate white linen suit, with a white shirt open at the neck, he was the picture of an urbane twentieth-century academic. Needless to say, the hand he extended toward Morgan held no sword.

"You are an admirer, Miss Swift?" he asked in flawless English as they shook hands. "We've met before? Were you one of my students? Sometimes it's hard to remember them all—though I'm sure I'd remember as lovely a young lady as you."

By now Morgan had had time to let his name register. "You underestimate your reputation, Professor," she said. "Anyone interested in astronomy, or archeology, or astrology, for that matter, knows your work on the Maya. As a matter of fact, I was planning on attending your lecture at the Mérida conference—before Tom persuaded me to come do some work down here."

"Tom is a master of persuasion," said the professor. "As you see, he persuaded me to come here too. But perhaps we will both be finished with our work in time for me to give that lecture. In fact, if all goes well, the lecture will be especially interesting. I may be able to announce a most important new discovery."

"A new find—on this site?" said Morgan.

"An amazing one," said the professor. "Perhaps it is too early to talk about it, but—"

At that moment he was interrupted by Sally's voice. She was standing in front of a large, brightly lit display screen that had attracted them the moment they entered. They had thought it was a TV set, but had discovered differently. Now Sally was declaring, "I tell you, it's *him*, in some kind of costume."

"What's the discussion about?" asked Tom.

"It *is* him, isn't it?" Sally demanded, pointing at the picture on the screen.

Morgan suppressed a gasp. On the screen was a picture of an ancient Maya ruler, a crown of feathers on his head, a sword in one hand, a severed head in the other.

It was the image she had just seen. And Sally was right—it was the image of Professor Hernandez.

The likeness was spooky, but it did cheer Morgan slightly. She told herself she well might have glimpsed it on the screen without knowing when she entered the room. That, not her power of second sight, might have produced her vision. The mind played strange tricks.

Her eyes traveled from the picture on the screen to the professor and back again as she tried to convince herself.

Meanwhile, the professor was saying, "It is an uncanny likeness, isn't it? But it really is not that extraordinary. As you may have noticed, many people in the Yucatán have the features of the ancient Maya. And this is especially true of the people of this particular jungle region, where I was born."

"You mean—you're a Lacandon?" Morgan said.

The professor smiled at the surprise in Morgan's voice.

"Strange to say, I am," he said. "I was born in a jungle village. But my family moved to the town of San Cristóbal de las Casas on the edge of the highlands when I was quite small, and I went to school there. I went on to college in Mexico City and then to Stanford University in the States with the aid of the Mexican government. As you may know, the government wants very much to integrate the Lacandones into the mainstream of modern national life, though I must say I am one of their very few success stories. Most Lacandones remain passionately attached to their old ways." The professor smiled. "But I should be grateful to them for that. Their language—the language I learned as a child—is virtually the same as in ancient Maya inscriptions. It has been invaluable in my investigations."

"And you've been invaluable in mine," said Tom. He turned to Morgan. "Wait until you see what the professor has come up with."

"I couldn't have done it without you—and your helpers," said the professor, indicating the display screen. "Your computer system is a marvel."

"It sure produces a great picture," said Sally.

"It's the highest-resolution graphics display I've ever seen," said Jenny.

"E. Z. has provided us with state-of-the-art hardware and peripherals," said Tom. "Want to see them in action?"

Morgan grinned at him. The more she saw of Tom, the more she was convinced he was the Tom she used to know.

"We couldn't stop you from showing us if we tried," she said. "You look like a a kid with your favorite toy."

"How right you are," said Tom. "Working with this system is the most fun I've had since I was a kid. Take this picture on the screen. Let me show you where it comes from."

He led them over to a large slab of stone brought in from the ruins outside. On it were badly chipped remnants of a bas-relief. Peering at it, Morgan could see that it well might have been the original of the picture on the screen. As she examined it more closely she could see faint hints of color on its surface indicating that it had once been painted. But Morgan's eyes were trained. The girls could see nothing at all.

"How could that picture come from *this*?" said Sally.

"Somebody has a lot of imagination," said Jenny.

"No imagination needed," said Tom. "We simply programmed the details and colors we found on the stone into the computer. Then we added what we know about other Maya portraits. Finally we asked the computer to project a picture of what the bas-relief would look like if it hadn't been damaged by a thousand years of wear. What you see on the screen is what the portrait looked like when it was new."

"Wow," said Sally. "It's like being in one of those time machines in science fiction."

"It's even better," said Jenny. "It's science, but it's not fiction."

"If you think that's good, take a look at *this*," said Tom, happily punching out a fresh computer command. "Here's what you kids couldn't see out there in the clearing."

The screen went dark. There was a humming sound. Then the screen lit up again.

"Fantastic," said Morgan. Her heart seemed to skip a beat at the vision suddenly before her.

Chapter 7

The city on the screen was breathtakingly beautiful. It was dominated by a huge, four-sided, flat-topped pyramid, with steps leading up the sides to a temple perched on its top. Nearby, an observatory thrust an awesomely tall cylindrical tower toward the heavens it was built to study. On a low rise of ground sat an ornately carved three-story palace, its interlocking courtyards filled with blossoming gardens and glistening pools. Down a highway made of stone was a huge stadium built around a long grass field lined by high walls. This, Morgan knew, was the field for *pok-a-tok*, a Maya ballgame played by two teams for the lives of the losers. After that, Morgan took in the other lesser pyramids and temples and aristocratic residences and countless statues and stelae, memorial slabs of carved stone.

The picture matched any vision that Morgan's gift of second sight had ever produced.

"You've got some computer there, Tom," she

said. "So that's what those ruins out there looked like a thousand years ago."

"That's just based on what we've uncovered so far," said Tom. "If we find more, I can punch it in, and the computer will expand the picture still further."

"One thing's missing, though," said Sally.

"What's that?" asked Tom, suddenly alert at the hint of anything wrong with his computer system. "I'm sure it can be fixed."

"People," said Sally. "I mean, a lot of people must have lived here."

"Only about ten thousand," said Tom. "But of course that was only a small part of the population the city served. In Maya civilization, a center like this housed only the nobility and priests, together with their soldiers and servants. Most of the people were farmers who lived outside the center in huts much like the ones they live in today. They came into town for religious festivals and for aid and advice from the authorities."

"You mean, they lived in the jungle out there?" said Jenny.

"Hundreds of thousands of them," said Tom. "Except it wasn't jungle then, but farmland."

"Boy, those Maya had it all together—for a while, anyway," said Sally.

"You must have found a wealth of artifacts," said Morgan, still dazzled by the sight of the city.

"I'll give you a look," said Tom. He snapped the computer off and led them into another room, larger than the first.

"I see what you mean about this place being filled to capacity," said Morgan. "It's a treasure house."

The room was jammed. There were statues, carvings, pottery, weapons, shields, and countless utensils.

Sally, though, was a shade disappointed. "Didn't you find any treasure? I mean, *real* treasure. You know, like gold and jewels. Or am I being hopelessly romantic?"

"Outside of the jade claw, we found nothing," Tom said. "It's a bit of a puzzle. We can be sure the place was full of riches, so we have to think it was looted."

"What you've found is valuable enough," said Morgan, eagerly examining an exquisitely decorated serving bowl.

"You haven't seen the most valuable find of all," said Tom. "Should I show it to her, Professor?"

"Certainly," the professor said. "Soon the world will know about it, anyway."

Tom led them to a glass case in the corner of the room. There, side by side, lay a series of sheets of what looked like crude paper covered with drawings and odd-shaped lines and dots.

"Is this what I think it is?" asked Morgan.

"It is—and it's intact," said the professor, beaming.

"Looks like some kind of book," said Jenny.

"An ancient Maya book," said the professor. "We call it a codex. Before this, there have been only three others ever found, and those in poor condition."

"The Maya weren't big on writing, I guess," said Sally.

"They wrote a great deal," said the professor. "But the early Spanish conquerors, eager to stamp out the Maya ways, burned all the codices they found. Only three escaped. Now, however, we have a fourth."

"So that's why you're here, Professor," said Morgan eagerly. "You're the best one in the world to translate it. Have you made much progress?"

"Excellent progress—with the aid of Tom's computer," said the professor. "I would not have believed how much help it could be. I merely programmed in the meaning of Maya hieroglyphs and numerical symbols. Then I fed in the contents of this codex. After the computer produced a translation, it was merely a matter of filling in the blanks and smoothing it all out."

"And what did you find?" asked Morgan, growing more eager still.

"As you doubtless know, Maya codices deal with astronomical records and astrological forecasts," said the professor.

"I know that," said Morgan. "That's why I'm so interested. Astrology is—kind of a hobby of mine."

"Well, then you *will* be interested in this codex," said the professor. "It is nothing less than an extraordinary system of complex formulas to determine the astrological portents of each day within a period covering thousands of years."

"You mean, it forecasts the future?" said Sally.

"Like a super fortuneteller?" said Jenny.

"That's right," said the professor, smiling. "The Maya had great faith in astrology. It inspired much of their constant investigation of the heavens."

"And these forecasts extend to the present time?" asked Morgan.

"They go much further than that," said the professor. "They extend many centuries into the future."

"Wow," said Sally. "Could I find out if I'm going to land a modeling job this summer?"

"And if I'll be accepted by M.I.T. when I apply next year?" asked Jenny.

"I'm afraid the codex won't help you that way," said the professor. "It appears to forecast only events in this particular city—with remarkable accuracy. It predicted the destruction of the city, though the date it gives seems a bit later than when the destruction probably occurred. It even predicted the city's rediscovery two years ago."

"And what about now?" asked Morgan.

"Now?" the professor said.

"What does it predict will happen here now?" asked Morgan.

"I must confess I didn't bother to work that out," said the professor. "I'm afraid I don't share your curiosity about the future. The past is what interests me."

"We could find out," Morgan suggested. "The computer should be able to do the calculations quickly."

"But I already know what the ancient Maya

would predict for the next few days, Miss Swift,"
said the professor, smiling.

"How?" asked Morgan. "And what?"

"As you may know, the Maya developed a
perfect 365-day solar calendar," he answered.
"It had twelve thirty-day months, with a special
five-day period, the Uayeb, at the end of each
year. We have now entered the Uayeb. The
Maya believed it was the unluckiest time of
year. According to them, we can expect one
thing only for the next five days: danger."

Chapter 8

Ancient wisdom or not, this has to be a lucky day, Morgan said to herself the next day as she finished dating a water jug that Tom had assigned to her.

The excitement of her work helped to dissipate the lingering doubts caused by the professor's prophecy, as well as the ones caused by her own flashes of foreboding on this trip. If some kind of trouble was ahead, she'd deal with it when it came up. Being scared stiff wasn't Morgan's style—especially when she had much more interesting things to do.

The water jug she was examining was of superlative workmanship and almost perfectly preserved. The colors of the painted animals that decorated it—a deer, a pheasant, and one of the jaguars seen everywhere in the carvings and paintings in this city—were still vivid. But what gave it special value was its age. It was nearly a thousand years old. Morgan had done a triple check with thermo-luminescence analysis to make sure.

Now just one thing to find out, Morgan thought as she checked the trace elements in the pottery against the composition of the local soil. The portable computer that Tom had furnished her with made it easy. There was no doubt—the jug had been made here.

I can hardly wait to tell Tom, she thought as she snapped the computer off. She was sure now that Maya civilization continued to flourish on this site for at least a hundred years after it had collapsed everywhere else. This city well might have been the last fortress of Maya civilization on earth.

She found Tom near the great pyramid, sifting through a heap of rocks. With him were Sally and Jenny. They had eagerly volunteered to help him and now they were doing their best to keep their attention on the rocks they were supposed to be sorting and not on Tom's handsome face.

His face brightened when Morgan reported her findings.

"Fantastic," he said. "We never suspected a city held out as long as that. Maybe it was because this spot is so remote."

"This place is a gold mine of information," said Morgan. "You come up with anything interesting today?"

"You could say I've found too much," said Tom, indicating the heap of rocks that he and the girls were sifting through. "A new trench near the pyramid turned up all these building stones. They must have come from the temple that was on top of the pyramid. We'll have to work up a new picture of what that temple looked like with the computer."

"Hey, look what I found," said Sally. She held up a rock. "It has a curving edge."

Jenny, working beside her, held up another rock. "This one has a curving edge too."

The same thought struck both girls at the same time. They put their two rocks together. They were a perfect fit, like pieces of a jigsaw puzzle.

"Great work," said Tom, and both girls flushed with pleasure.

"There must be more of those building stones around here," said Morgan, beginning to look around. "If they were all part of the same piece of construction, they probably fell to the ground close together."

An hour later they had found enough of the rocks to see that they formed the edge of a large round hole—a hole built into some kind of wall.

"Maybe it was an entrance to something," said Jenny.

"But what kind of entrance would be perfectly round?" said Sally. "I think it was a window."

"The Maya had no glass, and no windows as we think of them," said Tom.

"There has to be an answer," said Morgan. She stared hard at the assembled building stones, trying to come up with a vision of their purpose. But she drew a blank. Her brows still furrowed in concentration, she turned to Tom. "I think it's time to play with your favorite toy."

"Funny, but I was thinking the same thing," said Tom. "Come on."

He and Morgan led the girls to the building housing the central computer. A different guard from the day before was by the door, but his rifle gleamed with the same mute menace.

"E. Z. wasn't kidding when he said he was heavily into security," said Morgan as the guard waved them in.

"With all the relics in here, you can't blame him," said Tom. "Private collectors and even a few museums would pay fortunes for them—no questions asked. Even the Indians around here know about the money to be made peddling relics. In a way, I'm almost glad we haven't found any gold or jewels. If we had, we couldn't even trust our guards—though E. Z. claims they're hand-picked. From the looks of some of them, they must have been hand-picked at a penitentiary."

At the computer, Tom took out a notebook and consulted some figures. Then he inserted a disk and punched in a series of commands.

"The machine is programmed to come up with probable configurations of the temple on top of the pyramid," he explained. "It already has all we know about styles of Maya architecture, and I've now entered our new estimate of building materials used."

"Good thinking," said Morgan. "When we see what the possibilities are, we can figure out how a circular opening could fit into them."

"Wild," said Jenny as the computer whirred and clicked. "It's as though the picture of the past we saw last night doesn't exist anymore, and the past is changing right in front of our eyes."

"It happens all the time in archeology," said Tom. "We're always coming up with new findings that make us throw out old ideas. For a long time we didn't think Maya rulers were entombed in pyramids, until one was found in the great pyramid at Palenque. We also thought that Maya peasants were nomadic—that instead of farming in one spot, they moved from place to place. Then satellite photos picked up the traces of hundreds of miles of ancient stone walls built to separate fields."

"So you can never be sure when you've found the truth," said Sally.

"All of science is like that," said Morgan. "That's why I love it. It makes you keep a permanently open mind."

Their discussion ended abruptly when a picture flashed on the screen.

Below the picture was a message: THIS IS THE ONLY POSSIBILITY INDICATED FROM STYLES OF MAYA PYRAMID TEMPLE ARCHITECTURE IN MEMORY BANK.

The screen showed a large boxlike temple on top of the pyramid. Thrusting upward from the rear of the temple room was a towering wall of stone with sides tapering to a rounded top.

"Looks like the Maya version of a sky-scraper," said Jenny, wide-eyed.

"It's a style of building that emphasized height," said Tom. "Typified by that towering wall on top of the temple. We call it a roof comb. But let's find out more." He punched out a query, and a series of numbers appeared below the pyramid. "The top of the comb was a hundred and seventy feet above the ground. It's the tallest structure on record."

"Now all we have to do is figure out where the round opening fit in," said Sally.

"Let's see what the computer says," said Tom. The whirring began again.

"It's going through its memory bank," he said.

It took five minutes for a reply.

"NO RECORD OF CIRCULAR OPENING IN THIS STYLE OF ARCHITECTURE."

"Back to square one," said Jenny.

"Not quite," said Morgan, looking hard at the picture. "Tom, do you know the diameter of the opening?"

"Sure," said Tom. "I figured it out before we got here. Twenty-four feet."

"And how wide is the roof comb?"

Tom queried the computer.

"THIRTY-FIVE FEET WIDE AT BASE. TAPERING TO TWENTY-EIGHT FEET BEFORE SEMICIRCULAR TOP."

"I thought it would fit—I could just see it," said Morgan.

"What would fit? I don't see—" Tom began. Then he grinned. "I get your drift, Morgan. You were a step ahead of me, as usual."

He punched away at the computer keyboard. A circular opening appeared in the roof comb of the temple, the curve of the opening matching the curve at the top of the comb.

"It sure looks right—at least from an aesthetic point of view," said Tom.

"It looks perfect," said Morgan.

"But it looks a little weird, too," said Jenny.

"Yeah, like a giant eye on top of the temple," said Sally. "It's kind of creepy. You think it was done for decoration—or what?"

"The Maya had a deep sense of beauty—but they were also a very practical people," said Morgan. "That opening must have had a purpose."

She looked at the circular opening, and like an eye it seemed to look back at her, unblinking, inscrutable.

Finally she shook her head and said, "I can't see it."

It wasn't until dinnertime that night that she could.

They all had dinner together—Morgan, the girls, Tom, the professor, and E. Z.—in E. Z.'s luxurious tent.

After the meal Tom said, "I'm turning in early, and I suggest the rest of you do, too. We should start working at dawn, to take advantage of all the daylight we can. This time of year, there's not much of it. We're practically at the shortest day of the year. The winter solstice."

That was all Morgan had to hear to suddenly exclaim, "That might be it!"

"What might be it?" asked the professor, pausing with a forkful of papaya halfway to his mouth.

"The answer to the mystery of the opening in the roof comb," said Morgan. Both the professor and E. Z. had joined the rest of them in wrestling—unsuccessfully—with the problem all through dinner.

"You reckon you found it?" said E. Z., putting down the tall glass of bourbon he had been drinking.

"It's worth checking out," said Morgan. "The opening faces a mountain to our southeast. That's where the sun rises at the solstice. And it's just the kind of thing that the Maya liked to celebrate. I have a hunch that the opening was designed to let the first rays of the solstice dawn shine through it."

"Hey, you might be on to something," said Tom. "In fact, they discovered a previously unknown temple in the ruins at Tulum by spotting where the first light of the winter solstice struck."

"My hat's off to you, little lady," said E. Z., raising his glass in a toast. "Now we have to find out where that special spot is. It might turn out to be something real valuable." He took a long swallow from his glass. "I can't believe that looters got all the gold and jewels."

Morgan looked at him sharply. There was something in his avid expression, something in his gleaming eyes, that brought back to mind the picture of a shark.

But that thought was interrupted by the professor. "It will take a long time to find it," he said. "The opening that provides the key has vanished forever."

"It won't take long—with the computer," said Tom, and the way he leaned forward, his mind already racing, reminded Morgan of a jaguar about to spring, already licking its chops at the feast to come. "I just have to input the height of the mountain, the height of the opening, the position of the solstice dawn. I can get together that data in a couple of hours. After that, it'll take about two minutes for the computer to spit out the answer."

"Do it first thing tomorrow," said E. Z., and Morgan noted the tone of command in his voice. E. Z. might claim Tom was in charge of this project, but E. Z. was clearly the one who gave the orders.

Tom, though, didn't seem to mind.

"No way I'm waiting until tomorrow," he said. "I'll do it tonight."

"Good boy," said E. Z. "I'm staying up with you."

"I'd like to, too," said Jenny. "It's really super what you can do with that computer, Tom."

"Me, too," said Sally, admiration shining from her eyes.

"You won't find me going to sleep," said Morgan, and she meant it in more ways than one. The air was charged with something more than excitement. It was as if invisible forces had been set in motion, forces that she could sense but could not see, strain as she might.

"I hate to fit into the stereotype of the lazy Latin American," said the professor. "But I'm going to bed. I think your findings will wait until tomorrow, and I need a fresh mind in the morning to deal with a particularly tricky inscription I'm trying to decipher." The professor rose from the table. *"Buenas noches. Hasta mañana."*

The professor went off to his tent, and the rest of them went to the computer building. E. Z. sat and smoked a long cigar, and Morgan and the girls looked at relics, while Tom gathered the data he needed from maps, astronomical charts, and the computer memory bank.

"Gather around, folks," he said finally. "Watch my pal do his stuff."

All eyes were glued to the screen as Tom punched out his last sequence of commands.

The picture of the entire ancient city appeared, with the new version of the pyramid temple. Then on the screen a line representing the dawn's rays moved from the east toward the temple. The line passed through the opening in the roof comb and—

Darkness.

On the screen. And in the entire building.

At the same instant there was the sound of an explosion from outside.

And then Tom's voice exploding in the darkened room:

"Oh *no!*"

Chapter 9

"*Guard!*" E. Z. bellowed in the dark.

Almost instantly a flashlight beam appeared. It revealed Morgan, the girls, and E. Z. standing in a bewildered group behind Tom. Tom, for his part, was staring bleakly at the computer.

"Somebody blew up the generator," said the guard. "Must have used a blasting cap from our supplies."

"We'll have to fly in another generator *pronto*," said E. Z. He turned to Tom. "Don't look so down in the mouth, boy. I've seen a lot worse things happen drilling for oil. We always manage to get the stuff out of the ground in the end. We'll have that computer going full blast in no time."

"The memory bank was full of vital data," said Tom, in a voice as bleak as his expression. "I was planning on transferring it all onto disk first chance I had to organize a system, but new stuff kept coming in too fast."

"Like I said, no sweat," said E.Z. "Soon as we

get the computer going again, you can do it then."

"Don't you *understand*?" said Tom. "When a computer is shut down in the middle of an operation, its memory bank is wiped clean. I mean, *clean*. Everything I put into it is gone— the new data about the dawn, the proportions of the pyramid, the layout of the city, all the rest. We're not even back on square one. We're on square zero."

"Not quite," said Morgan, who had long since figured this all out.

"What do you mean?" said Tom.

"We've still got the best computer system in the world—our brains," she said, and her brain did feel very much like a computer now, clicking away to come up with answers fast.

"Yeah?" said Tom. "Try working without the computer. For instance, try figuring out where the sunlight coming through the roof comb opening would hit the ground. You could get the answer easy—in a few weeks."

"It should just take two days," said Morgan. "Less than two days, in fact."

"Impossible," said Tom, still looking mournfully at the darkened screen.

"It's very possible," said Morgan. "In case you

forgot, the winter solstice is the day after tomorrow. If we rig up a dummy tower on top of the pyramid, complete with a circular opening, we'll be able to see for ourselves where the light falls."

Tom looked at Morgan and shook his head, grinning. "I should have known better than to tell you something's impossible, Morgan. I remember the last time I did it, back in Santa Monica. I said there was no way you could ride the waves after that big storm, remember?"

"I remember," said Morgan, smiling at the memory.

"Next thing I knew, you were swimming out to sea," said Tom.

"And you were right behind me," said Morgan.

"Right behind Sam, anyway," said Tom. "He was after you like a shot. He was the only one who stood a chance of beating you in a race anyway."

Jenny and Sally leaned forward to catch his words, but Morgan cut him off brusquely. "We can talk about old times later. Right now we have to get organized for tomorrow. And it might be nice to figure out who blew up the generator while we're at it."

"I wonder what the professor's been doing all this time," said E. Z. "It's kind of hard to buy his story about wanting to go to bed early."

"The professor?" said Tom, startled. "You can't think that *he*—"

"He's one of *them*," said E. Z.

"He's a world-famous scholar," said Tom. "Morgan will back me up. She knows his work even better than I do."

Morgan would have liked to support Tom and defend the professor.

But she remembered her vision of the savage Maya ruler too well.

All she could say was, "I can't see what motive he would have."

"Like I say, he's one of *them*," said E. Z. "I never did meet a native I could trust—and I've been in every godforsaken primitive country in the world."

At that moment, from the darkness behind the guard with the flashlight, they heard the professor's voice.

"What happened?" he asked. The flashlight wheeled to shine on him, and followed him as he came to join the group. "I was sleeping when somebody smashed something in my tent. I just barely got a glimpse of a figure running out, and

I found my computer smashed to bits. Then I heard an explosion from this direction, and I came to find out what was happening."

"Glad you showed up," said Tom warmly. "We can use your help. You're the only one who speaks the Indians' language. Maybe you can find out if they know anything—something they might not reveal in Spanish."

"Of course," said the professor. "But you still haven't told me what happened."

"Sabotage," said E. Z. "A terrorist attack."

"Terrible," said the professor. "I'll be glad to help. I'll start first thing tomorrow."

"I reckon right now is the time to start," said E. Z., "before they have time to cook up some fancy story."

He took the flashlight from the guard and led the group out of the building. But they had barely stepped outside when another guard brought the news:

"Sir, the Indians—they've packed up and gone."

"Well, I guess that settles who did it," said E. Z. with grim satisfaction.

"The Indians?" said Tom incredulously. "But why?"

"Outside radical agitators must have riled them up," said E. Z.

"Outside agitators—here?" Morgan shook her head.

"Believe me, little lady, those agitators are everywhere, stirring up trouble," said E. Z. firmly. "I know what I'm talking about. This kind of thing has happened to me before."

"Anyway, it doesn't much matter who did it," said Tom. "What matters is, there goes our plan. No way we can put up that tower tomorrow."

"I tell you, boy, you're turning into a defeatist," said E. Z. "No damn bunch of natives is going to wreck *my* plans. My security people are just going to have to lay down their guns and pick up tools. They'll do it okay. I pay them good money. And they don't belong to no union."

"What tower are you talking about?" asked the professor.

Tom explained the plan, and the professor nodded.

"Very ingenious, Tom."

"Give the credit to Morgan here," said Tom.

"My compliments, Miss Swift," the professor said, looking at her appraisingly. Almost in spite of herself, Morgan felt a glow of pride. There was a kind of authority in the professor's gaze that made his approval matter to her. "You are clearly a woman to be reckoned with."

Morgan's glow faded. Suddenly she was not sure if she was being complimented or threatened. She looked into his eyes, but they were as dark and impenetrable as the night around them.

"I just hope we can do it," said Morgan. "Tomorrow is going to be a long, hard day."

"I am sure you can do anything you set your mind to," the professor said. He looked at his watch. "Until tomorrow then. Good night."

"I can hardly wait until tomorrow," Jenny said as she and Sally walked back to their tent with Morgan.

"And the break of day after that," said Sally. "I wonder if we'll really find anything."

"Don't get too excited to sleep," said Morgan. "The next couple of days, there's not going to be much chance to rest."

Back at their tent, it came as no surprise to find the shattered remains of the computer Tom had supplied Morgan with. She shook her head sadly. It had been fun while it lasted.

She watched the girls climb into their sleeping bags, grateful that they hadn't been harmed in the night's explosion of violence. Then she crawled into her own sleeping bag and switched off her flashlight.

"Good night," she said to Sally and Jenny.

"Night," they answered.

A moment after Morgan closed her eyes, she was asleep. But her sleep was troubled by dreams—dreams that merged into one another like a kaleidoscope of nightmares: a shark swimming at her, jaws open, as she frantically tried to protect the girls and herself; a Maya ruler waving a bloody sword in one hand and carrying a severed head in the other; and then, most vivid of all, a gigantic jaguar, fangs exposed, claws bared, springing at her with a roar, while the girls screamed.

Then Morgan realized her eyes were open.

The tent flap was open too, and moonlight was streaming in.

And in that moonlight, the head of a jaguar, the claws of a jaguar, the roar of a jaguar, and the screams of Jenny and Sally as the jaguar sprang.

Chapter 10

Morgan had never dealt with a jaguar before. She could only do what she did in any tight spot. She moved fast.

She rolled over, sleeping bag and all, to shield Jenny and Sally. In the same motion her legs in the sleeping bag shot up, then out, to catch the jaguar in the snout.

Except it wasn't a snout.

And it wasn't a jaguar.

Her kick smashed into something hard. A mask.

The figure that recoiled backward, partly from the force of the kick and partly from the shock of surprise, did not have four feet but two—it was a man wearing a jaguar mask.

The claws that extended from his fingers were longer than any jaguar's. Morgan could see now that they were made of metal, glittering menacingly in the moonlight.

She struggled to free herself from the sleeping bag to defend the girls and herself from those claws. But she didn't have to.

Giving another hideous roar, a perfect imitation of a jaguar's rage, the figure dragged one set of claws across the dirt floor of the tent, repeated the gesture, and raced out through the opening.

Morgan's first impulse was to go after it. Then she remembered Sally and Jenny.

"Are you okay?" she asked them.

"What was that *thing*?" Sally's voice was squeaky with fear.

"Some guy doing a pretty good imitation of a jaguar," said Morgan.

"And to think I was worried about snakes," said Jenny, trying to control her trembling. "Little did I know."

"Little do we still know," said Morgan. "Let's go see what we can find out."

She found her flashlight and led the girls out of the tent. All over the site, flashlights were shining. From the air it would have looked as if a swarm of fireflies had gone crazy. But the flashlights weren't really necessary. An enormous full moon lit the site almost as bright as day.

Morgan heard Tom's voice. "Morgan. Jenny. Sally. Thank God you're all okay."

Morgan turned toward him and saw that he was not okay. She turned her flashlight on him to see more clearly. He was wearing a pair of jeans

83

he must have pulled on, but his upper body was bare—except for a T-shirt that was wrapped around his upper right arm. Its white fabric glistened bright red with blood.

"You're hurt," Morgan said.

"Just a scratch," Tom said.

"Don't play macho with me," said Morgan. "That looks bad. It should be taken care of."

"In a minute, Florence Nightingale," said Tom. "First I want to check out the damage. From the sound of it a lot of people have been hit—and those claws were mean."

"A jaguar man went after you, too?" said Morgan.

"There must have been a pack of them," said Tom.

"What in damnation is going on?" shouted E. Z. He was coming their way with three of his guards, all carrying flashlights and pistols.

"A group of men wearing jaguar masks attacked the camp," said Tom. "They try to get at you, E. Z.?"

"Wish they had," said E. Z. "My security men would have had a nice jaguar shoot. But whoever those terrorists were, they must have known about the firepower around my tent."

By now his entire crew had gathered around him.

"Count heads, Clem," E. Z. ordered.

A minute later Clem reported, "All present and accounted for, sir."

"Except for one," said Morgan.

"The professor," said Tom, with concern.

"I told you he was one of them," said E. Z.

The flap of the professor's tent hung open. Tom led the way inside and played his flashlight around the interior.

The professor was gone. The only trace of him was a ripped-off pajama sleeve lying on the dirt floor next to a moist patch of earth. Tom picked up the sleeve. Once it had been pale yellow. Now most of it was reddish brown.

"Blood," said Tom. He shone his flashlight on the damp patch of ground. "More blood." He shook his head, his mouth tight. "Just what I was afraid of. Like you said, E. Z., he was one of them. But he was with us. That must have made them want to get rid of him most of all."

"Reckon he's still alive?" said E. Z.

"From the amount of blood spilled, I wouldn't count on it," said Tom. "Anyway, there's no way to find out. That jungle out there is their home. If we tried to follow them, we'd be lost in minutes."

"But who are *they*?" asked Sally.

"A local native tribe," said Tom. "I should

have picked up a warning signal when the workers took off. They must have been told to get out."

"But *why*?" wondered Jenny. "What could they have against us?"

"Maybe it has something to do with that circular opening we discovered," said Morgan. "Maybe we're getting too close to something they don't want us to find."

"That's a real interesting notion," said E. Z. "But I still prefer a simpler explanation. They just don't like us Americans. Some Yankee-hating radical has stirred them up against us."

"What about this then?" demanded Morgan, shining her flashlight on the ground. Two strokes of a claw had scratched a crude cross in the dirt. "The same sign was scratched in our tent."

"In mine, too," said Tom.

"I don't get it," said E. Z. "These here savages aren't Christians, are they? What are they doing with a cross?"

"You tell him, Tom," said Morgan.

"When the Spanish conquered the Yucatán, they tried to convert the natives to Christianity," said Tom. "But it didn't work. All the natives did was take the Christian symbol of the cross and make it part of their old religion. They called it the Talking Cross, because they thought their ancient gods actually spoke to them through it."

"And what really happened was that their leaders were using the crosses to dictate to them," Morgan added. "They concealed themselves near the crosses, which were huge, towering structures, and in the voices of the 'gods' they demanded that the people drive out all outsiders. As a result, over the centuries there was one violent uprising after another. The last one ended less than a hundred years ago. And apparently in this jungle, the Talking Cross still speaks—and is still heeded."

"Well, this is one outsider that there cross isn't going to drive out," said E. Z. "All it's done is make me mad—and more than a mite curious. If what we're getting close to is worth them natives running away before payday and then attacking us, it's worth us going all-out to get our hands on it. You with me, Tom?"

"I haven't come all this way to turn back now," said Tom. "But I don't think we should ask Morgan and the kids to run the risk. Those natives are still out there."

"No risks, no rewards," said Morgan. "I'd never forgive myself for missing a major find.

But Jenny and Sally are a different matter. I think it would be a good idea if they took you up on your offer of a deluxe tour of the Yucatán, E. Z. I can meet them in Cancun at the end of the vacation and fly home with them."

Sally and Jenny started to protest, but Morgan quickly silenced them: "Sorry, but you're leaving here on the first helicopter out, and no ifs, ands, or buts. Nothing is sillier than not being scared when there's a real danger around—and believe me, the danger around here is very real. Any doubts I had about that are all gone now." She turned to E. Z. "What about it, can you get them out of here?"

"First thing tomorrow," E. Z. promised. "My compliments, little lady. Both your courage and your concern do you a heap of credit."

Jenny and Sally looked at Morgan and saw that it was useless to argue. It would be like asking her to change the grade of a test after she had marked it.

The two girls looked at Tom and felt twinges of regret. Being around him had been great while it lasted.

He must have sensed that regret.

"I'll see if I can come with Morgan to Cancun," he said. "We can all spend a couple of days on the beach together."

"Is that a promise?" said Sally.

"Cross your heart?" said Jenny.

"Right." Tom grinned. "Though making any kind of a cross doesn't appeal to me much right now."

"Come on," said Morgan. "No time to waste on long good-byes. Let's get some *sleep*! Tomorrow is definitely going to be a busy day. We'll all have to be up early."

Morgan's words were truer than she imagined.

It was pitch dark when she awoke in her tent. The moon had set but the sun had not risen. From outside came the unmistakable din of a helicopter.

"Stay here—I'll check this out," she said to the girls, who had woken, too, groaning protestingly.

By the time Morgan left the tent, the sound of the helicopter was receding in the distance. She saw flashlights around the helicopter landing pad, and then saw that there was only one helicopter there, where before there had been two.

At the landing pad she found E. Z., Tom, and four armed men. She glanced at the four men and saw that they were the same men who had accompanied them from the yacht—E. Z.'s personal security force.

"The whole damn crew has lit off from here," said E. Z. with disgust. "They came to me and claimed that all this violence wasn't part of their contract and they were going. I'd bet my life that some kind of labor organizer was among them and stirred them up."

"I wish you had woken me up when they came," said Tom. "Maybe I could have talked to them, persuaded them to stay."

"I promised to pay them triple time to stay— and if they wouldn't listen to that kind of money, they wouldn't listen to anything," said E. Z. "I'm just glad that Sam, Clem, Hans, and Charlie here aren't scared of a little trouble, are you, boys?"

The four guards answered with grunts, and the most talkative of them, the big, bald one named Charlie, said, "We ain't running out on you, boss."

"I also hope you boys aren't scared of a little work," said E. Z. "We're going to have to work nonstop tomorrow—or I should say, today." He looked at the faint glimmer of light now appearing around the mountain rim to the east. "By the time that there sun comes up again, we're going to have to have a tower built, and every hand in camp is going to have to build it."

"And the girls?" said Morgan, already knowing the answer.

"No way to get them out now," said E. Z. "Not until we find what we're looking for. Better tell them that, Miss Swift."

"I'll do that," said Morgan. "And I'll tell them one more thing, too."

"What's that?" asked E. Z.

"To do what I'm going to do," said Morgan. "To be on their guard, every second from here on in."

Chapter 11

"Well, we did it," said Tom with satisfaction, gazing up at the tower on top of the pyramid. "I have to admit, there were a couple of times yesterday when I thought it would come crashing down on our heads."

Standing far above them was the tower, hammered together out of wood taken from almost every piece of construction on the site, and crudely propped up. The opening near its top was only a rough approximation of the perfect circle of the original, and the entire makeshift structure would never stand up to a strong wind. But it was the best they had been able to do working through the day and far into the night, and it would stand up as long as it had to, to do its job. After today it would be needed no more.

"Thank the Lord there are no clouds," said E. Z., peering at the brightening sky.

"Here she comes," said Morgan, squinting eastward at the mountain rim where the first glow of dawn was changing to the glare of the sun.

"It's like sitting in the dark, waiting for a movie to begin," said Sally in a half-whisper.

"Except we don't know what the show will be," said Jenny.

All of them—E. Z., Tom, Morgan, the girls, and E. Z.'s four security men—watched the sun clearing the mountain until the glare made them turn their eyes away. Then they swung their gazes westward, where the sunlight now fell.

"Now we'll see," breathed Morgan as the shadow cast by the tower grew distinct. Like a giant finger it extended along the ground and up the base of a mountain that rose on the western side of the site. Then, in the tip of that finger of darkness, as the sun fully cleared the mountain and sent its light streaming through the tower opening, a circle of blazing light appeared.

Morgan ran for that circle of light, ignoring the branches that scratched her bare arms and legs as she went up the gentle slope of the mountain base. She stood in the center of the light, waiting for the others.

Tom was the first to reach her.

"I knew you were good at distances—but you're quite a sprinter, too," he said, panting from his uphill run.

Jenny and Sally came next, finishing in a dead heat.

"It's like looking for a pot of gold at the end of the rainbow," said Jenny.

E. Z. was close behind, showing surprising speed. He clearly had muscle below his slightly soft exterior.

"I was going to say the same thing—except I don't see a sign of the stuff," he said. Shaking his head, he looked at the undergrowth that covered the slope.

"As an archeologist," said Tom, "I suggest we dig below the surface of this mountainside."

"As an old oil prospector, I agree," said E. Z. He called to his men, who still stood near the pyramid. "Move it! I'm not paying you to sun yourselves! Grab your picks and shovels and hustle your butts over here."

"Wish I could help," said Tom. "But this arm—" He looked down at the heavy bandage on his upper right arm.

"I'm paying you for your brains, not your brawn, Tom," said E. Z. "Besides, this might turn out to be a dry hole."

But when the men arrived, E. Z. eagerly grabbed one of the shovels they brought, and Morgan grabbed a pick.

Jenny and Sally were tentatively picking up tools, too, when Morgan said, "Let me see your hands."

Both of them showed Morgan hands covered with broken blisters from using hammers and saws the day before.

"I think you've earned a rest," Morgan said, and the girls didn't argue. They stood aside and watched as the clearing of the undergrowth began.

By noon, though, the girls had been put to work. The sun was burning hot now, and Jenny and Sally were making frequent trips to fetch water.

"Hey, what about a lunch break, boss?" one of the security men pleaded.

"Just keep on going until I say to knock off," said E. Z., digging his shovel into earth softened by Morgan's pick. "I'm afraid that's going to be pretty soon. We're about ready to hit solid rock."

"We've just done it," said Morgan as the tip of her pick clanged loudly.

"Well, that about cuts it," said E. Z. with disgust. "Tom, you shouldn't have got my hopes all up with that mumbo-jumbo of yours."

"Let me borrow that shovel," Morgan said to E. Z. "It's always worth taking one last look at things."

"Like you thought, it's solid rock," said E. Z. as Morgan shoveled the dirt away.

"It's rock, all right—but look." Morgan, on her hands and knees now, brushed off the rock surface.

Tom was on his hands and knees beside her.

"The rock has carvings on it," he said.

"Well, that's nice," said E. Z., his voice loaded with sarcasm. "That's what we really need—a few more carvings on some kind of marker."

"It's not a marker," said Morgan. She pressed her ear against the surface of the rock and tapped it with her pick. "It's hollow. It's some kind of door."

"That's more like it," said E. Z., and he kneeled beside her. "Let's get it open." He pushed at it with both hands. "No dice."

"We'll have to rig up a system to lift it out," said Tom.

"We don't have the time to waste," said E. Z. He gave the slab one last shove, then stood up. "Clem, Hans, go get some blasting caps."

"Can't do that," Tom said. "This isn't oil drilling, E. Z. These carvings are precious. They can tell us a lot."

"I can tell you something, too," said E. Z., motioning for his men to get going. "We got all the carvings we need. You still haven't figured out what a lot of them mean, as it is. It's time to get our hands on something different. It's time to hit real pay dirt. We're so close I can practically smell it. I've got a nose for it."

"But you can't—" Tom began.

"I *can*," E. Z. said. "I'm paying for this expedition. And what you pay for, you own. Maybe they don't teach you that in the university, but you learn that in the real world right fast enough."

"Maybe you won't have to blast," said Morgan, who had continued brushing off the door until it was completely exposed. "If it is a door, there must be a way to open it."

The others clustered around her as she examined the rock slab. It was covered with carvings depicting a procession of Maya dignitaries carrying heavily laden platters up a slope. They were viewed from the side, but their destination was carved so that it was seen from the front: the gaping wide-open jaws of a giant jaguar head.

Sally pointed to one of the platters. "That what I think it is?"

"A human skull," said Jenny. "Gross."

"And look how realistic they made those jaguar jaws," said Sally. "They even hollowed them out, like they were just waiting to eat you up."

"Let's see what happens if I give the jaguar what it wants," said Morgan, and put her hand into the jaws. "There's some kind of handle inside. Maybe if I pull it." She shook her head. "Won't budge. But maybe with two hands." She put her other hand inside.

"You need more muscle," said E. Z. "Clem, give the little lady a hand."

"Let's see what the little lady can do by herself," said Morgan, gritting her teeth. "It's beginning to give!" She kept pulling. "I think I've pulled it out as far as it will go." She withdrew her hands from the jaws. "Let's see what a push will do now."

E. Z. eagerly helped her as she pushed at the door, and a triumphant smile broke over his face as the door swung open, its hidden locking device released.

"Must be something real valuable in there, if they went to that much trouble to protect it," said E. Z.

"One way to find out," said Morgan. She took a flashlight from the utility belt she wore around her khaki shorts, switched it on, and stepped through the doorway, into the darkness beyond.

E. Z. was right behind her, his flashlight out too. The others followed.

They were in a tiled tunnel whose sides were covered with mosaics depicting more of the same procession shown on the door: an endless stream of Maya bearing offerings, all moving down the tunnel.

At the end of the tunnel, a hundred feet away, was another entranceway.

"Brrr," said Sally, when the first flashlight beams hit it.

"At least it's wide open," said Jenny.

"Is that good or bad?" said Sally.

What they saw was familiar—but not comforting. It was the same design that was carved on the stone door to the tunnel—but many times larger.

A huge jaguar's head with jaws opened wide.

Jaws big enough to walk into.

Chapter 12

E. Z. didn't hesitate. He wasn't afraid to walk into the jaws of the jaguar; he practically elbowed Morgan out of the way to be first.

"Hidden away like this, it has to be some kind of treasure chamber," he said as he stepped into the darkness.

Then, before the others had time to follow him, they heard his voice from the other side. It was a voice filled with angry disgust.

"Shoot! Some treasure!"

Led by Morgan, the others went through the jaws—to see what E. Z. stood staring at. A large subterranean pool in a high-vaulted cave.

Morgan shone her flashlight down at the water.

"It looks fresh, not stagnant," she said. "It must be fed by an underground stream."

"What do you think the Maya used a place like this for?" wondered Jenny. She dipped her hand into the water and let it run through her fingers. "Brrr, it's like ice water."

"I'm no archeologist, but I can answer that," said E. Z. "The Maya bigwigs must have used it as their private place to cool off on hot days. There weren't no air conditioners in them days." He shook his head bitterly. "So this is our big discovery. An old Maya swimming hole. This whole project is jinxed. Far as I'm concerned, we can give this godforsaken place back to the natives. They deserve it."

Morgan and Tom exchanged glances.

"You tell him," Morgan said.

"You're right about not being an archeologist, E. Z.," said Tom.

"I don't need you to tell me that," said E. Z. "Matter of fact, I'm getting sick and tired of you telling me a lot of things. I remember how you told me what a valuable find this place would be. What do we have? Some beat-up rocks. Some water. And a whole lot of my money down the drain. I might as well have put it in a bag and dropped it into this here pool."

"You might have—if you were an ancient Maya," said Tom, unable to repress his grin any longer.

"What do you mean?" asked E. Z.

"A pool like this was a sacred place to the Maya," said Tom. "Often they dropped valuable offerings to the gods into it. There have been some incredible finds made at the bottoms of pools. And who knows what's at the bottom of this one?"

"We're going to know—and quick," said E. Z. Already he was kneeling, his face close to the water. "Can't see a thing. The water must be deep." He stood up and slapped his thigh in frustration. "If only we had some dredging equipment. That's the one thing I never imagined we'd need here. I'll have to fly some in."

"*Whoa* there, E. Z.," said Tom. "Remember, we're not sure there *is* anything down there. I don't want you accusing me again of leading you astray."

"Say, Tom, sorry about that," said E. Z., laying a soothing hand on Tom's shoulder. "Guess I kind of lost my head—you know, disappointment and all."

"Sure," said Tom. "In this business, we all feel that way sometimes, angry and ready to quit, before we get back to work. It comes with the territory."

"Speaking of getting back to work, we have to find out what's down there," said E. Z. He shone his flashlight at the mirror-like surface of the pool.

"If only this arm wasn't injured," said Tom.

"What do you mean?" asked E. Z.

"I've got my diving gear back in my tent," said Tom. "I brought it up from Isla Mujeres."

Morgan cleared her throat. "May I make a suggestion, gentlemen?"

An hour later Morgan was back at the pool in a wet suit, with an air tank on her back, goggles on her face, and a high-intensity underwater flashlight in her hand.

"Good luck," said Tom.

"Good hunting," said E. Z.

"Good-bye for now," Morgan said, and lowered herself into the water. She submerged her head, and with a sweep of her arms and a scissor kick with her legs, she moved out of sight underwater.

"Wow," said Sally as she watched the rubber fins on Morgan's feet vanish beneath the surface. "I don't think I'd like going down there."

"Yeah," said Jenny. "It's like one of those pools in a science fiction flick where some prehistoric monster is waiting."

Moving swiftly downward, Morgan followed the beam of her light ever deeper into darkness. She had never made a dive like this. She had the feeling she was going where no other living thing had ever gone before. There was not a sign of life as she approached the pool bottom.

Then she saw it in front of her eyes.

Not a sign of life—but a sign of death.

A hideously grinning skull.

Relax, she told herself. *You shouldn't be surprised. You know the Maya sometimes sacrificed more than precious objects to their gods. Keep a grip on yourself, Morgan. Never panic underwater.*

She checked herself to make sure her breathing was smooth, her muscles under complete control, then continued along the bottom of the pool. She didn't flinch at the other skulls she found, or spend precious time examining the jewels and other artifacts she scooped up and put in a bag at her waist as she glided through the water.

This is what it must be like in outer space, she thought as she worked. *All by yourself, far from everything familiar, moving through the unknown. Maybe I should have tried out for that astronaut program back in Colorado when I was offered the chance, despite all the red tape. I could have—*

Then she looked up from an ancient, jewel encrusted headpiece she had just thrust into her bag—and froze, her muscles rigid with shock, her breath trapped in her lungs.

You're seeing things, Morgan.

But even as she told herself that, she knew she wasn't.

She saw it too clearly, as clearly as when she had first seen it in a flash, when Tom had showed up on the boat to Isla Mujeres.

It was as close now as it had been then—two feet away from her face.

A giant jaguar, snarling, poised to spring.

Chapter 13

"What's taking her so long?" Jenny said, worried.

"It's not really that long," Tom said, trying to sound reassuring. But he was worried too.

Sally peered at the glasslike surface of the water. "What could be happening down there?"

"Here she comes!" said E. Z., spotting the first ripple that signaled Morgan's return.

E. Z.'s eyes lit up when he saw the bulging bag at Morgan's waist, then gleamed brightly at the jewels and golden ornaments she emptied out onto the rock floor.

"You've brought in a gusher!" he exulted.

"Wait until you see my real find," said Morgan. "You won't believe your eyes. I couldn't believe mine, until I examined it."

"Didn't you bring it up with you?" asked E. Z., his hands full of jewels.

"It's much too heavy," said Morgan. "We'll need a rope and a block and tackle to haul it off the bottom."

Instantly E. Z. turned to his men. "You heard the little lady. Move it!"

"I hope your big find is nothing like this," said Jenny, pointing to a bone that lay among the treasures spread out before them.

"I'll let it be a surprise," said Morgan, smiling.

E. Z.'s men followed his orders fast. Within an hour they had rigged up a hoist. Again Morgan went down to the pool bottom, this time with a pair of ropes.

As soon as she returned to the surface, she shouted, "Haul away! But take it slow! Don't jerk the lines! We don't want to risk any damage!"

There was none.

Ten minutes later the group stared wide-eyed at Morgan's find as it was set down on the rock floor, dripping with water.

A giant jaguar, snarling, about to spring— exquisitely sculpted from a huge block of flawless jade.

"It's in perfect condition," said Sally, hardly daring to breathe.

"Except for this," said Jenny, and pointed at where the jaguar's front claw was missing.

"I have a hunch Tom can fix that," said Morgan.

"I've got the same hunch," said Tom. From his pocket he took the jade claw he carried as a good luck piece. It fit perfectly. The jaguar was complete.

The jaguar was not the only thing totally restored, thought Morgan. Her confidence in Tom was, too. She was sure now where her vision of the snarling jaguar had come from. It had come from the claw he carried in his pocket—the claw of the jaguar that had been waiting almost a thousand years to be found.

"This must have been one of the greatest treasures in the Maya world," said Tom, holding the claw in place. "They valued jade above all other precious stones."

"Forget the Maya," said E. Z. "This has to be one of the greatest treasures in *our* world. No telling how much it's worth. I know one sheik who would give half his oil kingdom for it, just so he could have something none of his royal cousins could match."

"Lucky it's us who found it," said Tom. "The Mexico City museum will devote an entire room to it alone. They might even name the room for you, E. Z. You'll go down in history."

"I hate to break the news, Tom," said E. Z., "but history is not what I'm interested in." He gave a nod to the four men who stood behind him.

They understood the meaning of that nod instantly.

A moment later Morgan, Tom, and the girls understood it, too, as they stared into the barrels of the glittering nickel-plated automatics that E. Z.'s men had drawn from their holsters.

Morgan, though, wasn't thinking about the guns. She was thinking about the smile on E. Z.'s face. That smile made her think of only one thing.

A shark about to strike.

I should have known, she told herself angrily. *I should have been on guard.*

Tom looked dazed. He shook his head, trying to clear it. "This doesn't make sense."

"It makes a lot of sense," said E. Z., and his smile grew even wider. "A lot of dollars and sense."

"But what do you need the money for?" said Tom. "You couldn't have backed this expedition for profit. I told you that I couldn't guarantee what I'd find."

"That was two years ago—when oil was thirty-two dollars a barrel," said E. Z. "I didn't need the money then—I needed to improve my public image after a spill off the California coast."

"I remember that spill," said Tom. "It killed off surfing for a year. Was that *you*?"

"It was one of my companies," said E. Z. "My public relations people told me I'd best do something real nice—and backing a big scientific project would get me some beautiful headlines, plus a pretty tax write-off for equipment I already had in Mexico." E. Z. shrugged. "The trouble is, headlines aren't what I'm after anymore. I took a big dive on a merger just before oil prices took *their* big dive. If I don't come up with big bucks fast, I'll get all the headlines in the world, when the banks foreclose on me."

"And what kind of headlines do you think you'll get when we spill the beans on you?" said Tom, too angry now to be afraid, or even to notice the guns pointing at him. "I know you think you can buy us off—but you're wrong. Money can't buy everything. These treasures belong to the world."

"You're wrong about the payoff I'm giving you," said E. Z., still smiling. "And you're wrong about the headlines. The only headlines are going to be about you being kidnapped by jungle terrorists. The employees I've sent back to Villahermosa have already told everybody about the danger here. And my men here will say what I tell them to say, just like they'll do what I tell them. They have often enough before. Right, boys?"

The men said nothing, but their ugly smiles mirrored E. Z.'s.

"And what do you think will happen when they find our bodies?" asked Morgan. "You'd be surprised what they can learn with autopsies."

Morgan wasn't interested in E. Z.'s answer. She was interested in gaining enough time to figure a way out of this trap—before it snapped shut for good.

E. Z. was only too happy to give her an answer, though. "Not much chance of an autopsy. Not for another few hundred years, anyway." He shone his flashlight on the pool. "And by then it'll be real hard to tell your bones from all the others down there."

"But there's something you haven't thought of," said Morgan.

"And what's that?" E. Z. asked, as not only he but everyone else looked expectantly at her.

She tried desperately to think of something else to stall E. Z. with.

She could only say, "You think I'd tell you?"

"You would if you could," said E. Z. "I know what you're trying to do. You want to kill time, hoping something's going to save your skin. I admire your spunk, little lady, but we've finished killing time. It's time to kill something else."

"This can't be happening," said Sally, barely managing to get the words out.

"It has to be a bad dream," said Jenny.

The two girls instinctively held hands, squeezing tight, as they looked into E. Z.'s merciless eyes.

"Look, the girls won't say anything back home if you let them go free," said Morgan. "I'll make them promise not to. You can trust them."

"They're just *kids*," pleaded Tom, and for the first time Sally and Jenny didn't mind being called kids by him.

"Too bad they'll never get to be grownups," said E. Z. "I didn't get where I am by trusting anybody. That's why I sent back all the employees I couldn't trust to Villahermosa—and why I made sure the kids stayed here. They already knew too much about our little treasure hunt. They should have let me buy them a nice vacation trip instead of coming down here—because it was a once-in-a-lifetime offer." Then his voice hardened. "I also didn't get where I am by letting anyone pull a fast one on me. Miss Swift, I would appreciate it if you and the others put out your flashlights and tossed them at our feet. I wouldn't want you to try anything foolish like shining them in our eyes and making a break for it."

Morgan gritted her teeth. E. Z. had read her mind. Her last hope of getting out of this jam had gone as dark as her flashlight now did. The flashlights clattered as they hit the rock floor at the feet of E. Z. and his men.

The only light now came from the flashlights trained on Morgan and the others.

All Morgan could see was the blinding blaze of those lights.

All she could hear was the pounding of her own heart.

Then E. Z.'s voice.

"Okay, boys, let's do it."

Chapter 14

Morgan refused to blink. She braced herself for the deafening blast that would be the last sound she would ever hear.

But all she heard was a series of startled grunts as she saw E. Z. and the others stagger and then fall, their guns and flashlights dropping from their hands as they went down.

The flashlights went out, and all Morgan saw then was the fading red afterglow imprinted in her eyes.

Then, suddenly, the darkness was lit by torchlight.

It's happened. I'm dead. This is what it's like, was all that Morgan could think.

She saw before her a figure that could not belong to the world of the living.

In the torchlight stood an ancient Maya ruler, with a crown of brilliant feathers on his head and a sword in his hand.

"I'm sorry for waiting until the last minute," he said. "I realize how frightening it must have been for you all. But I wanted to be absolutely sure how guilty these men were before I passed sentence on them."

Beside him, a native lowered a torch to illuminate the bodies of E. Z. and his four men. They lay motionless.

Tom shook his head, dazed.

"Professor Hernandez," he said. "You're dead."

"Not exactly." The professor smiled.

"You faked it all—the signs of struggle, the blood," said Morgan. "I had a feeling I should do an analysis of the bloodstains, but I didn't have a chance. What was it? A pig? A chicken?"

"A chicken," said the professor. "And a very good dinner it made that evening."

"But why did you do it?" said Tom.

"Perhaps Miss Swift would like to tell you," the professor said. "She seems to have grasped the situation nicely."

"You wanted a way to join the natives in the jungle without our realizing it," said Morgan. "You must have learned all you wanted to about our activities in camp."

"*Very* good, Miss Swift," said the professor, nodding. "Perhaps you have some more information as well."

Morgan shook her head. "That's as far as my deductions go. You'll have to fill us in on the rest, Professor."

"Come, let us go back outside," said the professor. "We will all be more comfortable there while I explain."

The professor and the group of natives with him led the way out through the jaguar jaws, through the tunnel, and out the mountainside entrance.

"We entered the tunnel when we saw E. Z.'s men bringing in the block and tackle," the professor said as they emerged into the sunlight. "I knew for sure then that you must have discovered the secret of the pool. My people and I stationed ourselves outside the opening to the cave. We were there watching while you brought the sacred jaguar to the surface. You were really never in danger from E. Z. My people are very swift and accurate with their blowguns."

He indicated the long tubes that the men with him carried, along with their bows and arrows.

"You mean . . . ?" said Jenny, glancing back toward the tunnel and feeling a sudden chill.

"I mean, E. Z. was a rat, but still I don't like to think of him and his goons lying there d—" said Sally, unable to say the word "dead."

"I don't think the professor's people went that far," said Morgan, though she wasn't sure herself. "When the natives hunt with those blowguns, they tip them with a paste that stuns the prey, not kills it. Am I right, Professor?"

"Right as usual, Miss Swift," said the professor, smiling. "The breadth of your knowledge impresses me more and more."

"That's nothing compared to the respect I feel for you," said Morgan, looking at him with frank admiration. "I knew you were a man of intellect, but I never imagined you were a man of action, too. You really took command of the situation."

The professor smiled, as though at a private joke. "You might say it came naturally to me, Miss Swift."

"Well, you certainly got us out of that jam," said Morgan. "Now we just have to haul E. Z. and his men back to civilization and put them in front of a judge. The Mexican government doesn't take art theft lightly."

"That won't be necessary," the professor said, and there was a new note of hardness in his voice, like a layer of rock that lay just below the surface.

"What do you mean?" Morgan asked.

"They don't have to be taken back to civilization," said the professor. "They *are* in civilization—*my* civilization. And they do not have to be put in front of a judge. They have already been judged. They are guilty. They have been sentenced also—to hard labor until they have seen the error of their ways and no longer threaten my people."

"Boy, with E. Z. and those creeps with him, that would take *years*," said Jenny. "*Decades*, maybe."

"E. Z. sweating in the jungle all that time—I almost pity him," said Sally.

"Enemies captured in battle become slaves— that is the penalty our law demands," said the professor. "And that is the sentence I must pass on them."

"Professor, I'm a little confused," said Morgan. "What law are you speaking of? And how can you judge these men?"

"It is my duty to administer the law of the Maya," said the professor.

"Your duty?"

The professor's voice grew deeper, more resonant.

"My duty as the Jaguar King."

Morgan, Tom, and the girls all drew closer together as they faced him.

118

"Look, Professor," Tom said. "All the work you've done on the ancient Maya. It's been a great contribution, but it must have been a terrible strain. I can see how you . . . I mean, maybe if you tried to, well, *relax* your mind a while . . . er, take a *break* . . ."

The professor smiled.

"No, Tom, I have not lost my mind—and this is no costume I am wearing," he said. "I *am* the Jaguar King."

Morgan looked at him.

She did not say that she now saw in the flesh what she had once seen in a flash.

She only said, "I believe you—but you do owe us an explanation."

"You're right, I do," said the king. "I will give you one, if you don't mind a short lecture on Maya history."

"Not at all," said Morgan. "After all, that's one of the reasons I came to the Yucatán—to hear you lecture."

"And this is the perfect setting for it," said the king. Using his sword as he might have used a pointer, he indicated the ruins around them. "Here I need no slide projector to show you where my ancestors ruled, or what happened to their glory."

"Then you know what happened?" said Tom

eagerly. "What brought their civilization to an end?"

"Sadly enough, I do," said the king. "Let us make ourselves comfortable, and I will tell you the story."

The king led them through the ruins to the towering pyramid. He sat down on one of the broad stone steps on its westward side, bathed now in the late afternoon sun, and the others sat around him. The natives, clearly alert to any sign that their ruler might want or need them, stood at a respectful distance.

"As you know, the Maya were divided into two classes," he began. "One was the great mass of people who farmed the land and provided food and labor. The other was the small group who provided them with leadership and wisdom and law and protection from hostile tribes and hostile nature. For centuries the leaders led well and were rewarded by their people's love, tribute, and loyalty. But increasingly the leaders concerned themselves with amassing wealth, pursuing pleasure, waging war—until when a great drought plagued the land, they merely advised the people to endure it, rather than helping them to survive. In area after area, the people rose against their rulers, killing them and destroying the civilization they created. I am

120

proud to say this city was one of the last to fall. My ancestors were not as corrupt as the others, and sincerely tried to help their people in their time of need." The king pointed with his sword at the entrance to the tunnel in the mountain. "Sacrificing all their wealth to the gods was their last great effort to bring the rains—and when that failed, there was nothing that could stop the farmers from overrunning the city."

"But your ancestors survived," said Morgan. "You're living proof of that."

"Yes," said the king. "They were wise enough to realize that if they gave up their palaces and lived among their people, putting their knowledge and wisdom at their people's service, they could survive. As you said, I am living proof that they did. I am the Jaguar King—as my son, when I have one, will be."

"But you're not a king—you're a history teacher," Sally could not help saying.

"Not that we mean that as an insult or anything," said Jenny, and quickly added, "Sir. Your Majesty."

"It was my father's command that I leave the tribe and enter the outsiders' world," said the king. "He and his council of elders decided that I had to learn what was happening in that world, for the source of our power has always been our knowledge, and that was where the greatest knowledge now lay. I was sent to San Cristóbal with a foster family to begin my education. And now it has made me king."

"Your father is dead?" said Morgan. "I'm sorry."

"No, he is very much alive," said the king. "But now that he sees our people and land threatened, he has passed the crown on to me. He says that only I now have the knowledge to do what is needed to save us from invasion and conquest."

"He sure was right," said Jenny. "You did a neat job of handling E. Z. and his goons."

"It was kind of rough on them—but I can see why you had to do it," said Sally.

"Unfortunately," said the king, "there is still one more threat I have to deal with."

"Threat?" said Sally.

"What kind of threat?" asked Jenny, looking around her and seeing nothing but the ruins silent in the blazing sunlight, and the group of Indians standing silent and motionless nearby.

The king was silent.

But Morgan answered for him.

"Us, kids," she said. "He means us."

Chapter 15

"*Us?*" said Sally incredulously.

"A *threat?*" said Jenny, bewildered.

"How?" asked Sally.

"To who?" asked Jenny.

"Perhaps you should tell them, Miss Swift, since I can see you appreciate my position—and my problem," said the king, looking at Morgan with new interest.

"I can understand the spot you're in," she said, and turned to the girls. "You see, if word of the discovery of this treasure gets out, the entire region will be overrun with fortune hunters. It's the kind of invasion that the pro—" She paused. "The king, I mean, doesn't think would be good for his people."

"It would be a disaster," the king said. "The way of life my people have maintained deep in the jungle would be destroyed. I would be the last of the Jaguar Kings. A civilization and a dynasty that have endured would be ended. It is my duty to defend it—no matter what the

123

means." He paused and looked at Morgan and the others. "Sometimes a ruler must act in the interest of his people even though he personally may regret what he must do."

Morgan swallowed hard. Would they be prisoners in the jungle? Or even worse? She remembered the Maya ruler she had seen in her vision. She remembered his sword dripping with blood.

"Perhaps there might be another way of solving your problem," she said.

"And what would that be, Miss Swift?" the king said.

Morgan's heart was pounding, her mind was racing, but she forced herself to speak calmly. "It's fortunate for us that we are dealing with the civilized ruler of a civilized people. I know you are a man of wisdom, as well as a man of power, and that you'll give a fair hearing to what I propose."

The king nodded. "What might your proposition be, Miss Swift?"

"We will promise not to reveal the treasure we have found—only the discovery of the city," said Morgan. "I'm sure Tom will agree to make that sacrifice."

"I hate to lose them—they're quite a find," said Tom. "But if it's a choice between dead relics and a living civilization, I'll go along with the plan."

"And I'm sure Jenny and Sally will give you their word too," said Morgan.

"We sure will," said Sally.

"You can bet your life on it," said Jenny, before she realized how that phrase sounded, and put her hand over her mouth.

"You can trust them, you really can," Morgan assured the king. She looked him in the eyes. It was like looking into two dark, bottomless pools. How she would have liked to be able to get below *that* surface—to find out what was happening in the depths.

But she and the others could only wait, hardly daring to breathe, while the king made up his mind.

Finally, after a minute that seemed to last forever, he spoke. "You are most persuasive, Miss Swift. And I thank you for giving me credit for being civilized, not to mention intelligent." He paused, and now there was just the slightest hint of amusement in his voice. "It is fortunate for you that you are right. A Jaguar King does not fall prey to panic, and a Jaguar King knows how to pass judgment. During my stay among you, I had ample opportunity to judge you and Tom and Sally and Jenny." His eyes passed over each of them, as if making a final decision. "I know that you are not enemies but friends. I know you will join me in preserving the living heritage of the Maya."

"We promise," said Jenny as they all let out a breath of relief.

"We sure do," said Sally.

"You don't have to reassure me," said the king. "I have already decided you can be trusted—and that is enough."

Sally and Jenny exchanged a glance. Their fear had changed to awe. This was what the word "majesty" meant. They had just heard a royal pronouncement, and both silently vowed never to betray the royal trust.

"Thank you," Jenny said.

"Thank you," Sally chimed in.

It was all they could do to keep from curtsying, which would have looked very odd, since both of them were wearing grimy cutoff jeans.

"I thank you, too—though I must say, it was nothing less than I expected from you," said Morgan, suddenly realizing that deep within her, she *had* expected it. She could feel the emanations of a wisdom greater than any she had ever encountered coming from this short, slender man who seemed to grow in stature with every word he spoke. "If you just tell us exactly what you want us to do when we return to civilization—*our* civilization, I mean—we will be happy to follow your commands to the letter."

"You will have to do little beyond what you just suggested, Miss Swift," said the king. "Merely report the findings of an ancient city, rich in artifacts, but looted of all treasures. By the time archeological work is resumed here, doubtless with the help of the Mexican government, the sacred pool will have been emptied of its valuables. They will be given a new resting place deep in the jungle. I am sure our gods will understand the move."

Morgan nodded. "I'll do exactly as you say, Your Majesty," she promised. The others nodded in agreement.

"I must say, Miss Swift, the more I see of you, the more I am impressed," said the king, and Morgan felt the full weight of his gaze. She felt he was asking her to meet that gaze, and she did. For a moment their eyes locked, and Morgan felt a current of excitement within her that she had not felt for a long, long time, not since—

She forced herself to blot out that memory and listen to the king's words.

"Miss Swift, if ever you tire of *your* civilization and seek another, you will always find a warm welcome here. My people and I have great difficulties to face. In the coming years we must survive in a hidden world, a world whose existence grows more precarious each day. To have someone like you among us, someone with your talents—and your character—would be of great value."

Morgan knew the question she was being asked—and for a moment, caught up by the power of the king's gaze, the authority of his person, she was not sure what her answer would be.

Then, with an effort, she shook herself free.

"Thank you," she said. "And perhaps someday ..." She paused, then went on. "But right now I have a job waiting for me back home, and plans of my own for the future."

The king gave her one last, long look, and nodded.

"Of course, Miss Swift," he said. "I had to ask—but I suspected what your answer would be. I can see how you value your freedom."

"You are a good judge of character," Morgan said. "I don't think your people have to worry, with you as their ruler."

In the moment of silence that followed, Jenny cleared her throat.

"I don't want to be rude or anything, bringing this up, but how do we get out of here?" she asked.

"With the helicopter knocked out and all," Sally added. "I mean, it's kind of a long walk through that jungle."

"I have a treat for you—an experience you *will* be able to tell your friends back home about," the king said. "A canoe ride on an uncharted river back to within walking distance of San Cristóbal. My people will do the paddling. It will both get you home, and clear them of suspicion as terrorists."

"And what about you?" Tom asked.

The king raised his eyebrows. "Me?"

"I mean, you, the professor," said Tom.

"Unfortunately, Professor Francisco Hernandez vanished in the jungle, perhaps abducted by mysterious terrorists," said the king. "He will never be seen again. A tragic loss."

"Certainly is," said Morgan. "I was really looking forward to hearing you read your paper at the conference in Mérida."

"Now, that *would* be a tragic loss," said the king. "I did prepare an impressive paper, if I do say so myself. Fortunately, Miss Swift, my effort does not have to be wasted. Knowing your interest in astrology, I think you would be an excellent person to read it in my place, after you found it among my possessions after my disappearance. It is written in English, since that is the language of the conference."

"I'm not sure I'm the right one," said Morgan, caught totally off guard for one of the few times in her life. "Tom would be better qualified."

"I think you are the right one," said the king, in a voice that allowed no further discussion.

"I'm sure you are, too," said Tom. "I don't know one sign of the zodiac from another."

"You'd be great," Sally said.

"As your students, we completely endorse your lecturing style," said Jenny.

"Well, if you kids don't mind seeing me turn into a teacher before vacation ends," said Morgan.

"We wouldn't miss it," said Sally.

"We'll be right there, cheering," Jenny said.

Chapter 16

Jenny was as good as her word.

Four days later, sitting with Sally and Tom in the packed auditorium at the University of Mérida, she joined in the enthusiastic applause after Morgan finished her reading.

Morgan had to gesture for silence several times before the noise level fell enough for her to deliver her final words.

"I thank you for your generous reception of this paper, not for me, but for the good, wise, and dedicated scholar who wrote it, Professor Francisco Hernandez. I know that if he were here, he would urge you to use this paper as a stepping stone to pursue further knowledge of the greatness of the Maya and their civilization. *Muchas gracias* and *adiós, amigos.*"

The next day it was time for Morgan to say *adiós* to another *amigo.*

"What are your plans now, Tom?" she asked as they waited at the Mérida airport for planes that would take Tom to Los Angeles, and

Morgan and the girls back to Boston.

"Well, after I write up my findings here, there are some interesting possibilities in the Upper Sudan—traces of a lost Egyptian city," said Tom. "Maybe you could join me there. The Egyptians were deeply into astronomy and astrology, too."

"I know—and maybe I will," said Morgan. "Summer vacation isn't that far away. Right now, though, I have to reconfirm our tickets. I'll be back in a minute."

Jenny and Sally watched Tom's face light up at the prospect of seeing Morgan again, and saw how his eyes followed her as she headed toward the ticket counter.

"Morgan sure is something," said Jenny.

"She sure is," said Tom, still looking in her direction.

"For a couple of minutes back there in the jungle, I didn't think she was coming out with us," said Sally. "I could see a thing kind of developing between her and the king. I think he definitely wanted her to stick around."

"Morgan Swift, Queen of the Jungle," said Jenny with a grin.

"The king wouldn't be the first one with an idea like that," said Tom. "Back in California, every guy on the beach tried to figure out how to get next to her. Me, too. If it wasn't for Sam, maybe . . ." His voice trailed off.

Both girls leaned forward—and started to speak at the same time.

Then Jenny said to Sally, "You go first."

"Say, Tom, we keep hearing about this guy Sam," said Sally, trying not to sound too terribly curious. "We don't like to pry into Morgan's mysterious past, but . . ."

"Well, I don't see how it would hurt," Tom said. "I'll tell you about Sam. He—"

At that moment the roar of a departing jet drowned out his voice.

And by the time the jet had soared into the brilliant blue sky, Morgan had returned.

Sally and Jenny looked at each other and shrugged.

They had been just a shade too slow.

They had solved as much mystery as they were going to on this adventure.

The public address system announced the boarding of the plane to Boston in Spanish and then English. Morgan and Tom gave each other an affectionate hug and Tom gave Morgan a kiss on the tip of her nose. Then Morgan said, "Come on, kids, let's go." And she moved toward the departure gate in her long-legged stride.

"We'll find out more some other time," Sally said under her breath to Jenny.

"We'd better be quicker next time," said Jenny.

"You kids still with me?" asked Morgan, stopping at the departure gate and looking over her shoulder.

Both girls nodded vigorously. They speeded up to join her as she went through the gate and across the runway to the boarding ramp of the waiting plane. But neither of the girls was thinking of the trip home.

They were both looking forward to the next time they would have to try to keep up with Morgan Swift.